TOO LONG SHE HAD DENIED THE PASSION IN HER NATURE . . .

"Look at me, Amanda."

The husky command with its intimate caress warned her not to, but she couldn't help herself. When she raised her eyes, he saw the surrender and the need at once. He took her lips slowly with a sureness that opened her soul like a crack in a dam. Then his lips sent sensual life flooding into every nerve cell of her body, like a roaring river that had been restrained too long. . . .

CANDLELIGHT ECSTASY ROMANCES™

A
FATAL
ATTRACTION

Shirley Hart

A CANDLELIGHT ECSTASY ROMANCE™

Published by
Dell Publishing Co., Inc.
1 Dag Hammarskjold Plaza
New York, New York 10017

Dell ® TM 681510, Dell Publishing Co., Inc.

Candlelight Ecstasy Romance™ is a trademark of
Dell Publishing Co., Inc., New York, New York.

ISBN: 0-440-12842-0

Printed in the United States of America

First printing—September 1982

To Our Readers:

We have been delighted with your enthusiastic response to Candlelight Ecstasy Romances ™, and we thank you for the interest you have shown in this exciting series.

In the upcoming months we will continue to present the distinctive sensuous love stories you have come to expect only from Ecstasy. We look forward to bringing you many more books from your favorite authors and also the very finest work from new authors of contemporary romantic fiction.

As always, we are striving to present the unique, absorbing love stories that you enjoy most—books that are more than ordinary romance.

Your suggestions and comments are always welcome. Please write to us at the address below.

Sincerely,

The Editors
Candlelight Romances
1 Dag Hammarskjold Plaza
New York, New York, 10017

CHAPTER 1

Home to San Francisco. Amanda Kirk looked out the window of the airliner at the city of her birth. A light fog lay over the city, blanketing the hollows and exposing the tips of the skyscrapers, making the "good, gray city" look like a drowning metropolis caught in a flood tide of gray mist. The Golden Gate Bridge blazed red in the rising sun.

The seat-belt sign flashed on and she clipped the belt around her slim body. Her severely tailored gray suit was unwrinkled, her red-gold hair still in the smooth chignon she had fashioned it into five hours ago in her apartment in New York City.

Outwardly calm, inwardly a mass of nerves, she brushed a tendril of hair away from her temple and tried to fasten her attention on the view outside her window. Red-gold lashes, long and lustrous, flickered against the cream of her cheeks. Her eyes were a deep green, a green that had once glowed with passion for life and love but now was as cool and icy as the depths of a mountain lake.

Coming to San Francisco made her remember Colin, and she didn't want to remember Colin. She had left San Francisco to forget him. She thought she had. She thought she had put him out of her mind and heart forever. But now she was here in the same city where he practiced law.

She supposed he had captured the heart of his new secretary with his flattering ways. Did she work late at night preparing briefs for him as Amanda once had? But, of course, Colin was married now. Perhaps Lisa had put a curb on his late nights.

For Colin had broken his year-long engagement to Amanda and in a month had made Lisa Wallingford his wife. Had Colin ever loved her really? She had spent long hours with him, and she had fallen deeply in love. He had professed to love her, but as she thought back on it now, she could see that he had been seduced by the thought of being engaged to a girl from one of the old, original families of San Francisco. Coming from the Midwest, Colin had been impressed with the tradition and dignity that still lingered in Amanda's family, even though her mother had died years ago.

She stared out the window as the plane circled the bay. The island of Alcatraz sat in the swirling currents of fog and water. She couldn't hear them, but she could remember the sound of the island's foghorns. It was the last sound she had heard when she had gotten on the plane a year ago to flee the hurt and humiliation.

Alcatraz. *We all live in a prison that we build in our minds.* It had taken her a year, but she thought she had escaped her prison of hurt and pain. Now it was all coming back.

The plane circled, the engines revved in that sudden stress of reversal. She braced herself and was thrown against her belt slightly. Then the plane stopped. She was on the ground at the San Francisco airport. She was home.

The flight attendant, a man, reminded her to watch her step. His eyes admired her as she unclipped her belt and stood up to readjust her purse on her shoulder. She was in a disturbed, uneasy, and unhappy state of mind. She was neither enthusiastic nor glad to be in San Francisco. It had been a night flight from New York, and she was beginning to feel the effects of her hurried departure. She wondered why she had given in to her father's urgent telephone call to come home for her vacation.

Carried along in the crush of the crowd, Amanda entered the waiting area on the lower level of the airport. Her father's working day had already begun. Would he be here to meet her? He hadn't been sure if he could. But as she gazed around the circular lounge, his tall, lean figure rose from one of the plastic dishes that passed for chairs. When he came close enough for her to see his face clearly, she knew why she had come. His skin had a pasty look, and his steps were awkward. His smile might have been painted on by an incompetent make-up man.

"Amanda." He took a step forward as if to grasp her by the shoulders. Then his hands fell away, and his arms hung limply at his sides. She took the initiative, putting her hands on his chest and raising herself up to place her lips on his cheek.

"How are you, Father?" she asked, trying not to think of what he might say if he gave an honest answer, trying to tell herself that he didn't look as ashen as she had first thought. She didn't succeed. A corrosive acid seemed to be burning him away from the inside.

When she stepped away to look into his eyes, he made a nervous movement with his shoulders. "Let's go pick up your luggage."

She walked along beside him, remembering how he had looked a year ago when she had left. He had been a youthful-looking fifty, with a healthy tan and the agile walk of a man who was out on the golf course regularly. Now he seemed to have lost the ability to coordinate his leg muscles.

At the baggage-claim area, he asked, "Are those yours?" pointing to the two blue suitcases that were coming toward them.

She nodded and reached for the larger one, schooling herself to hide her concern about his appearance. But she was shaken to the core. He looked ill! "I'll take it," she said, grasping the handle before he could reach it.

He picked up the small overnight case with a rueful smile. "You're a liberated woman now, are you?"

"I've learned to look after myself, Dad," she said. *But what has happened to you?*

Her father turned away from her searching eyes and strode toward the glass doors. She swung into step beside him, knowing full well he would deny it if she asked if anything was wrong.

"I've been worried about you, Amanda," he said. "New York is big and unfriendly, and you hear such stories. . . ."

The automatic doors slid open, and they walked out into the warm sunshine. "San Francisco has some of the same problems, Dad," she replied. "I've learned to be careful."

They threaded their way through the parking lot to halt beside a blue hatchback car that was unfamiliar to Amanda. It was one of the newer, smaller models. Her father lifted the fan-shaped trunk to place her cases inside. His face averted, he closed the lid and said, "I've often wondered if I shouldn't have made you stay and face the gossip down. Now it will begin all over again."

"Why should it?" Amanda asked, shrugging. "Anyway, I'll be gone in two weeks."

The wind lifted strands of Maxwell Kirk's hair and spread them over his forehead. He raked them back with an impatient gesture, his eyes filled with sadness as he gazed at her. "I was hoping . . . I thought I might persuade you to . . . stay home for good, Amanda."

"You know I can't do that, Dad," she said gently. The smell of the sea reached her, tangy and nostalgic. "It . . . it just wouldn't be possible." His mouth tightened and the lines around it went deeper. She regretted her words, but she couldn't take them back. She couldn't make her home in San Francisco, he had to realize that. Perhaps it would have been better if she hadn't come home at all.

But there was his physical appearance. She felt disturbed as she watched him climb wearily behind the wheel of the car. She slid into the passenger seat, not knowing where to begin. Her father turned north and headed toward the city. A small sigh escaped her as she relaxed against the seat.

"Jet lag?" he asked, glancing at her as he guided the car down the busy highway.

"I think so," she said, seizing on the excuse. "It's supposed to be worse traveling from east to west. I had to get up early, and rushing to the airport probably didn't help matters any." She turned to look at her father's profile. Color had come back into his face, but he still had the look of an unwell, burdened man.

"How's Susan? Is she still enthralled with the latest love of her life?"

"She . . . she says they're going to be married," he said slowly.

Amanda sat up and stared at him. "Married! In her last letter, she told me she was registered for the Art Institute this fall."

"I know," Maxwell Kirk said huskily. "I guess I'm not sure just exactly when she changed her mind. I . . . I've been thinking about other things. She had hinted she was getting serious about this fellow, but I brushed her aside when she tried to talk to me about him. Now she's told me she's engaged and they're going to be married very soon."

"But, Dad, she's still very young—"

"I know that. And they won't wait. The young man is wealthy and eager to marry her. They go out dancing and dining almost every evening, and I'm afraid Susan is caught up in the glamor of it all. The reality of married life will be something quite different."

"Maybe if she didn't see so much of him . . ."

Her father's mouth twisted wryly. "What do you suggest I do, lock an eighteen-year-old girl in her room every night?"

Amanda shook her head. "No, of course not. But if you talked with her now . . ."

"In the last three days, I've talked until I'm hoarse," he said, gripping the wheel, plainly frustrated at the memory of those conversations and his own male ineptitude at dealing with his youngest daughter. "But it hasn't done any good. It's too late."

He turned the car onto California Street, and she heard the thump, rumble, and clang of the cable car. Ahead of them, Nob Hill rose, its hodgepodge of mansions attempting to maintain their dignity among the young upstarts, the new high-rise apartment buildings springing up everywhere in San Francisco. The Mark Hopkins Hotel towered benignly over it all just as always. Several more turns and they pulled up in front of the unfamiliar apartment building that was now Maxwell Kirk's home. He had moved just after she had left. Now he parked temporarily outside the building in a vacant space and set the wheels of the car against the curb.

Was it Susan then that had given her father that look of death warmed over? "Dad," she said, "Susan is of age. If this David loves her and she loves him, there's nothing more we can do."

Her father made a sound and shifted in his seat to lay his arm over the wheel of the car and stare at her. "But suppose he doesn't love her? Suppose he's only leading her on with talk of marriage as Colin did to you—"

She paled, and he made an awkward motion with his hand. "Amanda, I'm sorry. I shouldn't have said that. But I'm afraid for Susan. I don't . . . I don't trust this young man."

She forced herself to a calm she didn't feel. "If you think it will help, I'll talk to her, Dad."

His face relaxed. "I knew I could depend on you." He got out of the car, and Amanda did the same, fighting down the pain. For a year she had struggled, trying to forget Colin. How many people would remember she was once engaged to the young and brilliant lawyer on his way to the top? How many people would remember that just after they had announced their engagement he had met Lisa Wallingford at a party and in two weeks had broken his engagement to Amanda and placed the same emerald ring on Lisa's finger? And Amanda, who had been Colin's secretary as well as his fiancée, had fled the city to find work on the other side of the continent.

A bored security guard nodded to them as they walked into the building and across an expansive red carpet to the elevator. The door closed behind them silently. She was thankful her father had moved. There were no memories here, no thoughts of nights in front of the fire eating popcorn with Colin, long, tender kisses on the couch. Here everything was new and luxurious to her when she stepped across the threshold. Aqua curtains hung in swags framed a window view of the bridge. The same color carpeting covered every inch of the living-room floor, and white-velvet chairs, looking elegant and totally unused, were placed around the room. A curving couch the color of seaweed sat in front of what must have been a facade of a fireplace. A mirror glimmered above the mantel, reflecting the bookcase unit across the room filled with a stereo and records. That, at least, was predictable. Susan would not be parted from her music.

Then she saw the girl's bright-red head. She sat on the couch and Amanda could see in the mirror that she held a fragile china cup and saucer in her hand. She leaned forward to set the cup on the low table in front of her rather quickly, and the two pieces of china rattled against each other in the silence of the apartment. Susan raised eyes dark with emotion to the mirror. Behind her, Amanda felt the stilled body of her father, waiting.

"Hello, Susan," she said. "It's good to see you."

"Hello, Amanda," came the reply in a strangely mature new voice. "It's good to see you, too. Did you have a good trip?"

"Yes, I—"

The suitcase was taken from her unresisting fingers. "I'll put these in Susan's room, Amanda," Maxwell Kirk said, and was gone down the hall before she could protest.

Susan rose at once. "Would you like a cup of tea before you unpack? Or would you rather have coffee?"

Amanda smiled slightly, feeling like a schoolgirl being

made comfortable by the dowager queen. "Tea is fine. Can I help you?"

"No, it's nothing." She disappeared in the same general direction as their father—and was relieved to do so, Amanda thought. Left alone, she slipped out of her suit jacket and tossed it over the back of one of the chairs. She wandered to the window to gaze out at the bay. Sea gulls made lazy circles around each other, and a few intrepid sailors were already out on the water, the white sails of their ships filling with the breeze that blew from the sea. *Flags blow east*, she thought, and wondered how often random phrases from her school days would come to her mind. She watched the boats skimming over the water like the birds overhead and longed for one moment to be out there where life was simple and free and good. One could move with the prevailing winds and let them take the responsibility for motion. She felt a strange reluctance to talk to Susan. She was ill-equipped to advise anyone about love.

"Tell Susan not to bother with dinner," Maxwell Kirk said as he crossed over to the door, his eyes pleading another message entirely. "I'll be working late. You girls enjoy your day. Get reacquainted. I'll be home about eleven o'clock this evening."

"So late, Dad?" Amanda protested, thinking he needed more rest, not less.

"I'm working on a special presentation, Amanda. I have to have it done in a week. I'll talk to you later."

"Yes, of course," Amanda said, but he had already let himself out the door.

Susan returned, bearing a tray with a teapot and a fragile china cup like her own. Setting the tray down on the table in front of the couch, she said, "Sit down, Amanda. Drink this while it's hot. Aren't you tired after that long flight?"

"Not really," Amanda said, moving toward the couch, thinking Susan would sit down beside her. But she didn't. She wandered over to the window and stood looking out across the city as Amanda had done. Though she was dressed informally in jeans and a yellow T-shirt, she looked vulnerable and young and yet as old as time in the way only a girl on the verge of womanhood can. Her auburn hair hung down her back in a loose curl. Amanda remembered how she used to comb that hair and braid it.

She took a sip of tea and tried to think how to begin. Susan expected it, she knew, which, of course, made it all the harder. The hot tea was comforting, but when she set the cup down, she had no more idea of how to begin than she had had before.

The quiet in the apartment grew. Susan swung around at last, startling Amanda. "I know Dad's talked to you. So would you please say whatever you have to say and get it over with instead of sitting there staring at me?"

Amanda rose. "I was just thinking it was a lot easier when all I had to do was remind you to brush your teeth." She reached Susan's side, but stood looking out over the city. "I've haven't said anything because I don't know what to say." She paused. "Getting married is a little more serious than having cavities. I'm not sure I could handle it."

There was a sound of indrawn breath and Susan turned to her with eyes that brimmed with tears. "I always hated it when you made me get back up out of bed to brush my teeth, but, oh, Amanda, I've missed you."

They stood in each other's arms, hugging, Amanda patting the girl's shoulder. "I've missed you, too, darling, very much." Amanda held her, wishing she could soothe away all the aches and pains for this young girl who was her sister.

Susan moved away to dig in the pocket of her jeans for a handkerchief. Amanda smiled, walked to her jacket, and pulled a white bit of lace from her own pocket. "You never did have a handkerchief either, did you?"

"I promised myself I wouldn't be like this," Susan said, wiping her eyes and blowing her nose with vigor. "I told myself your coming home wouldn't make any difference." She lifted her head and said with a choked voice, "And it doesn't, Amanda. I'm still going to marry David."

"All right," Amanda said calmly. "Tell me about him."

"We love each other," Susan went on, Amanda's words not registering, "and we don't see any reason to wait. David can well afford a wife."

"Dad said he was wealthy. That's why he's so worried, I guess."

Susan heard that. "He shouldn't be," she said fiercely, walking over to the couch and throwing herself down on it. "It's because of Dad that we—"

She stopped speaking abruptly, and Amanda frowned. "What do you mean—it's because of Dad that you're getting married?"

"Forget it," Susan said flatly. "It isn't important."

"But—"

"It isn't, Amanda." She stared at Amanda defiantly.

Mystified, Amanda tried another track. "Well, if he's going to be my brother-in-law, the least you can do is tell me a little bit about him."

"David?" Susan's eyes lit up. "He's tall, about six two, and he has blue eyes and the most beautiful black hair and a marvelous sense of humor. . . ."

19

Amanda smiled at the look in her sister's eyes and crossed the room to sit next to her. "He sounds too good to be true. Where did you meet him?"

"At the Art Institute. I've been going Friday evenings for lessons, you know, ever since last fall. Anyway, I was late this one Friday. I was running down the hall and I came around a corner and ran right into him." Susan pulled her knees up and clasped her arms around them, staring in front of her, her eyes misty with remembering. "My drawing pad went flying and my charcoals scattered all over the floor." She smiled at Amanda. "It took quite a while to get everything picked up. Of course, he helped."

"And while you were picking things up, he said, 'How about a cup of coffee after class,'" Amanda finished, smiling.

"Actually," Susan said, grinning, "I never made it to class at all that night. We went for coffee right away. He ordered pie and we talked and talked. We both said afterward we knew that day we loved each other."

"And you've met his family?"

Susan dipped her head and rested her small, pointed chin on her knees. "No."

A shiver of alarm went through Amanda. "But, surely, if you're planning on marrying the man, you should meet his family at least once before the ceremony."

Susan looked directly at Amanda. "I know that, Amanda, and so does David. But . . . well, he's already tried to introduce me to them once. And he doesn't want to do it again. He doesn't want me to get hurt."

Amanda frowned. "I don't understand. Why would you be hurt?"

Susan sighed and unfolded her legs. "It's a long story. You see, David's brother doesn't want him to marry.

20

David went to him last Christmas and told him he was going to bring me home and introduce me to his mother, but Reid absolutely—with a capital *A*—forbade it. He laughed at David, Amanda." Tears glittered in her eyes. "He told David he was a damn fool for thinking of getting married at his age. Amanda, David is twenty-one, and old enough to marry. And he told him he should enjoy life before he settles down. By that, he means see a lot of different women." She got up restlessly, her face flushed with anger. "Because that's what *he* does. Reid Buchanan changes women with his ties. David says his affairs never last more than a few months or so." She paced the floor in front of Amanda, her words tumbling over one another. "He told David not to see me anymore, and I suppose he thought that would be the end of it. But David's stubborn, too." She threw herself back down next to Amanda and ran her fingers through her hair. "Reid Buchanan doesn't even know me, Amanda, but he told David I *had* to be marrying him for his money." Susan's eyes shone with the beginning of tears. "He's a cynical, arrogant—"

"That name seems familiar," Amanda said, trying to divert her.

"It should," the other girl retorted bitterly. "His picture is always in the paper because he's heading up some committee or attending some premiere with an actress from Los Angeles who flies in just to be with him for the occasion." Susan's lip curled. "He doesn't have to come to them, they come to him."

Amanda remembered. It had been just after she had discovered Colin's desire to break off their engagement that old Mr. Buchanan had died, leaving the running of a large conglomerate to his eldest son. Colin had handled the probate of the estate and had become Buchanan's legal

21

counsel. Reid Buchanan had even been in the office once or twice, she remembered now with clarity. She had been curious about him because he had been written about frequently in the press, touted as a whiz-kid, one of that breed of men who had everything—wealth, youth, and sexual appeal combined with keen intelligence. The press had given his sudden elevation to power many columns of space with all the Cinderella overtones they could muster. She had not been impressed with Mr. Reid Buchanan. She had thought him a singularly hard and unfeeling man with gray, flinty eyes and the kind of personality that would be expected of someone who gambled with the lives and fortunes of other people.

"That Reid Buchanan," she murmured.

"Do you know him?" Susan asked.

"Only by sight and reputation," she said dryly. "What about David's mother? Doesn't she have something to say about all this?"

Susan shook her head. "I don't know. She has a heart condition and has to avoid excitement. She lives on a ranch in the foothills of the Sierras. David doesn't see her much, and he hasn't told her about us." She sighed. "She's the only reason David and I aren't already married." She looked at Amanda, her eyes eloquent. "David wants to do the right thing, and so do I. We don't want an open break with Reid—David works for him—and it would upset their mother very much. But I don't know how much longer we can go on like this. David wants to get married, and I want to be his wife. Why should we wait forever?" She rose to her feet and began to pace again. "We should just stop worrying about everyone else and do it. Mexico is close—"

"Susan—" Amanda began, alarmed.

"We've tried, Amanda," she said earnestly, dropping to her knees in front of the table next to Amanda. "David has tried again and again to talk to his brother. But Reid Buchanan will not listen."

Amanda protested, "But, sweetheart, if you do this—if you run away and marry secretly—you'll still have to face everyone when you come back. David's brother and our father, too. He'll be very disappointed and hurt." She thought of her father's gray face. "And you have no way to judge what Mrs. Buchanan's reactions might be. She could suffer an attack from the shock."

"Oh, God, Amanda," Susan said, burying her face in her hands. "I couldn't live with that. I don't know what to do. David and I have talked about it so many times."

Amanda thought rapidly. "Suppose . . . suppose I went and talked with him, with Reid Buchanan. He would surely listen to me."

Susan lifted her head and laughed with bitter amusement. "What makes you think so? If you could catch him between meetings and plane trips—and women—he wouldn't listen to you any more than he did to his brother. He's the feudal baron. No one dares to contradict him."

Amanda shook her head. "He's just a man, sweetheart, a man with heavy responsibilities."

Susan stared up at her. "And one of those responsibilities is being head of the Art Council. Dad has a bid going to that council on the reconstruction of the old Art Museum next to the bay." She looked up at Amanda. "It's up to the council to award the contract."

"And you think an altercation beforehand with Reid Buchanan would spoil Dad's chances of getting it?"

"I don't know," the younger girl said, frowning. "I'm just afraid—"

23

"And you're worried about that along with everything else," Amanda said, her eyes watching Susan with tender regard. "Sweetheart, Reid Buchanan may have gotten where he is by being his father's son, but from what little I saw of him, I'd guess he'd be the last person in the world to let a personal situation influence a business one."

Susan made a choked sound in her throat. "Wouldn't he just? I don't think he'd stop at doing anything if it furthered his own interests. And he's *interested* in keeping me out of David's life. Right now, David's in the Orient because Reid wanted him there." She raised her head and gave Amanda a straight look. "But he can't keep us apart forever. David is almost ready to tell him to take his job and stuff it!"

"Susan—"

Susan jumped to her feet. "If we have to leave San Francisco and . . . and go live in a hovel, we'll do it! We have the right to live our own lives," she finished dramatically.

Amanda rose and slipped her arm around her sister's waist. "Before you do anything quite that drastic, let me at least try to see David's brother. We don't have anything to lose, do we?"

Susan turned to her, her eyes wide and troubled. "Amanda, you can't do it. You can't handle him."

Amanda smiled. "I've no intention of handling him. I'll only talk to him. After all, what can he do to me? He really can't eat me, can he?"

"He'll think of something, Amanda, I know he will," Susan said ominously.

Two hours later, Susan was as pessimistic as ever as she sprawled on the yellow coverlet of her bed and watched Amanda comb her hair in front of the mirror. The older girl had taken a shower, and then, at Susan's suggestion, changed into a wheat-colored wool dress that clung to her slender hips and let her hair fall loose and free to her shoulders.

"There's no use hiding your charms under a bushel, Amanda," Susan had said practically. "You're beautiful, and you might as well look it. Reid Buchanan won't look at you twice, let alone listen to you, if you go in that practical suit with your hair pulled back like a frigid frump."

Amanda knew Susan was right, but she felt a complete fraud. The dress and hair were not her. She turned back to the mirror and leaned forward to touch a wand of brown mascara to her lashes. *The better to see you with, Mr. Buchanan,* she thought wryly. Tiny flecks of gold sparkled in the green of her eyes. The droop of her eyelids gave her a slightly erotic look. She fastened gold loops in her ears and touched her mouth with a soft pink color.

"There," she said, standing back from the mirror. "Do I look all right?"

Susan sat up and folded her legs under her. "You look fantastic, Amanda." She studied her sister speculatively. "Did you ever find anyone in New York you liked?"

Amanda turned from the mirror. "I've gone out with a few men. Why?"

"I . . . I just wondered, that's all." She laughed softly. "I guess I never thought I would be married before you were."

Amanda shrugged and went to the closet for her light coat. "That's the way things happen sometimes."

"I still wish you weren't going," Susan said, reverting to her former apprehension. "I've got a funny feeling

25

about it somehow. And you must be tired from your trip
—"

Amanda shook her head. "That shower revived me.
Don't worry, darling. I'll be back before you know it. And
I'll plan on having a nice long nap this afternoon."

A cool wind ruffled the collar of her coat as she stepped
from the apartment building and walked to the cab that
stood waiting for her at the curb. She gave him the address
on Market Street that Susan had gotten for her and
climbed in. She braced her arm against the seat in front
of her to take the roll forward down Nob Hill. How long
it seemed since she had ridden over the steep streets of San
Francisco like this! It was a gorgeous morning, now close
to eleven o'clock, and the streets were filled with cars and
people enjoying the June sunshine. The taxi stopped for a
red light and a man dressed in a dark business suit strode
in front of them on the crosswalk. She was brought soberly
back to the present. What difficulties would she encounter
trying to see Reid Buchanan? Maybe she was foolish even
to attempt it. He was a busy executive and no doubt
monitored his appointments carefully or had his secretary
do it. There was a good possibility she wouldn't see him
at all. But she had to try. She had to, yes, even enlist his
help in preventing Susan and David from running away
and beginning their married life in exile from their families. She knew what it was to be in exile. She had been in
exile for a year.

The taxi rolled past the Wells Fargo Bank in the round,
the Crown Zellerbach skyscraper, the Shell Oil Building.
It came to a stop at one of the older, more prestigious
buildings, which was not a skyscraper, but nevertheless a
highly prized location. She hadn't remembered Arthur

Buchanan's company as having such an important address, but her mind had been on other things. If Western Associates had grown in the way everyone had expected it would, she supposed that success was expressed in the clean brick facade and the huge plate-glass door. Inside, all was bright modernity. The elevator that took her to the top floor was fast and quiet.

It was astoundingly easy to find her way around. The glass door labeled R. Buchanan was neither guarded nor locked. She hesitated briefly, then opened it, her heart pounding against her ribs. She was being silly to feel that way, she knew, but if she had been given a choice she would have turned around and left that elegant office suite and never put one foot in it again. Three women sat at wide, spacious desks in a well-lit, comfortable room. Cream-colored carpeting inches thick and walnut paneling fairly screamed executive success. One of the women sat at a switchboard at Amanda's left. Another was searching through the top drawer of a row of filing cabinets that stood along the back wall. The third kept a typewriter clicking.

The woman at the switchboard wore a soft silk blouse with a bow at the throat, which gave her a well-groomed, efficient look. She was about thirty, Amanda thought. At last she raised her head and looked at Amanda.

"Yes?"

"I'd like to see Mr. Buchanan," Amanda said, pleased to hear how coolly steady her voice sounded.

"When is your appointment?" the woman asked, scanning her face, trying to place her, then running her eyes over Amanda's coppery hair.

"I don't have one," Amanda informed her calmly.

A mask slid down over the woman's face. "I'm sorry,"

she said, with not one trace of regret, "Mr. Buchanan doesn't see anyone without an appointment."

Well-versed with the protective techniques of secretaries and receptionists, since she had used them all herself, Amanda's eyes dropped to the telephone receiver dangling on the console in front of the woman. "Then may I speak to him on the phone?"

"I'm sorry," she said again. "He's in conference all morning, and he will be leaving the building soon to catch a plane."

"I need to see him before he goes," Amanda stated clearly, and then said, "it's about a member of his family."

The silence that fell in the room was immediate and tense. The receptionist raised an eyebrow and said, "I'll call his secretary. If you'll just have a seat over there."

She pointed to the row of leather chairs. Amanda walked to one and seated herself, self-consciously aware that somehow she had succeeded in dropping a bombshell. What had she said?

The receptionist spoke in a low tone into the phone, her conversation punctuated by frequent looks at Amanda. At the end of the conversation, the woman replaced the receiver and nodded at Amanda with carefully noncommittal eyes. "I've relayed your message."

Within seconds, the door flew open. A man stood there, a tall, lean man with a set to his jaw that told Amanda he was extremely angry. In cold, incisive tones, he demanded of the receptionist, "Where is she?"

The receptionist nodded in Amanda's direction, relieved to divert his attention away from *her,* Amanda thought. She rose, a slight flush on her cheeks, her natural poise the only thing sustaining her. His eyes moved insolently over her, following the slim curves of her body under her coat down to the delicate instep of her heeled sandals. Amanda met his mocking gaze with cool eyes.

She remembered him. He looked no older, the dark hair still shone like black silk. There was an abundance of it lying casually around his face. He towered over her five seven by several inches. What was he, six three? At least. He took a step toward her as if determined to subdue her with his superior height and strength. She did not retreat as she longed to do, but stood her ground. She was determined not to let him see that he frightened her. It took every ounce of her self-control to do it, to meet those gray eyes steadily. There was no doubt about it. Reid Buchanan was a man to be reckoned with. He was infinitely disturbing—formidable and male and frightening because he was so . . . sexual. She was tremendously aware of the hard force of his male body and held motionless by his cold, intelligent eyes.

"What's this about a member of my family?" he asked grittily.

This time her voice was husky. "Would it . . . would it be possible to have a word with you in private, Mr. Buchanan?"

"Damn you!" he cried, startling her out of her wits, grabbing her by the shoulders, his hands iron hard on her bones. "If you're here to threaten me like that punk boyfriend of yours, I'll kill you!"

She stared into his angry face, trying to think. In desperation, her brain supplied the answer. Someone had threatened his or his mother's life recently. And she had had the ill fortune to give the impression that she meant to do the same.

Coldly she said, "Take your hands off me, Mr. Buchanan. I have no intention of harming you or your family. I am not an extortionist." Then, because she was afraid he would leave without hearing her out, she said quickly, "I want to talk to you about David."

His eyes changed, became hooded. They slid over her hair and smooth cheeks contemptuously. He released her, so abruptly that she almost fell backward. She righted herself just as he turned his jacketed back to her. "I've wasted time. See to it that I'm not bothered again by this glory seeker."

Anger shot through Amanda like flame through tinder. She stepped forward, caught him by the arm, and turned him toward her with a strength born of her fury. "You listen to me for just one minute, Mr. Buchanan. If I sought glory, I certainly wouldn't start with a self-centered man like you. You may think you're the only one whose family has ever been endangered, but you're not. You're endangering my family, too. You could help me if you'd take a minute to listen. But, no! You're too damn caught up in your . . . your conglomerates and your . . . your wheeling and dealing. You . . . I . . ." Amanda ran out of words.

She stared up at him, her fingers gripping his arm. There was a silence in the office, as if the other women were holding their breaths. Nothing in Reid Buchanan's mouth or eyes gave Amanda a clue to his thoughts.

"Do you have a name?" he said coldly.

"Amanda Kirk," she said automatically, her breathing quickened from her angry outburst.

"Is it Miss Kirk?" he said in exactly the same frostbitten tone.

"Yes," she said, matching his cool brevity.

"Miss Kirk, would you mind very much releasing my arm?"

She let go of him at once. He lifted the same arm she

30

had held to flick back the cuff of his shirt and look at the heavy gold watch he wore. "I'm lunching at the Mark in forty-five minutes, Miss Kirk. I'll meet you there."

Still flushed with anger, she shook her head. The Mark had been a favorite haunt of Colin's. "No," she said clearly. "I don't want to have lunch with you. What I have to say won't take that long."

There was an indrawn breath as the women gasped collectively. A muscle moved in Reid Buchanan's cheek as if he were having difficulty in controlling his emotions.

"Miss Kirk," he said coolly. "You've asked for a portion of my time today. You've already delayed the negotiations of my meeting this morning by several minutes. At two o'clock I'm leaving for Madrid to—in your words—wheel and deal. So if your need to see me is so great, cancel *your* luncheon date with your current man friend and dine with me."

Amanda clenched her teeth. More than anything else, she longed to tell him to take a flying leap into the bay. But she thought of Susan and swallowed her urge to lash out verbally. Instead, she said coolly, "Twelve o'clock then, Mr. Buchanan."

His mouth lifted in a cynical smile. "High noon, Miss Kirk."

CHAPTER 2

Amanda crossed the marble floor of the Mark Hopkins Hotel lobby and found a chair opposite the big floor-to-ceiling windows that faced California Street at an oblique angle. The sun would warm her there, and she had a view of the door so that she could rise and join Buchanan when he entered the foyer. There was a lounge and bar at the opposite side of the room where he might expect to meet her, but she wanted to greet him in the bright light of the sun, not the seductive darkness of a bar.

She relaxed against the chair and loosened her coat, her cheeks still glowing with anger. She hadn't even cared that the three women must have thought her tremendously cheeky to ask to use the telephone to call a taxi. A reluctant nod gave her permission to pick up the receiver. The three of them pretended to be very busy, but she knew they were listening for her announcement of her destination to the dispatcher. She had aroused their curiosity, which was natural enough under the circumstances, she supposed. Their boss was a virile and attractive man who would always interest a woman, regardless of her age or marital status. And, poor things, they would probably never learn the truth of the matter. To say that Reid Buchanan didn't

32

look the type to have cozy chats with his employees was probably the understatement of the year.

The warmth of the sun began to relax her, and she took advantage of the chair's high back to lift her face and close her eyes and let its warm glow pour over her. No, she thought, Reid Buchanan would never come into the office as Milton did, breezily good-natured, perching on the corner of her desk to ask about his appointments for the day. But then Milton was a theatrical agent who had once been bitten by the acting bug himself and still wore the unconventional purple-satin shirts and denim pants he loved. His wasn't the image of the urbane businessman. Yet that was what he was, and his ability to sort the gold from the dross and find genuine talent had made Amanda marvel more than once. They had a good working relationship; she grateful to him for giving her a chance at the job after a long search for employment in New York, and he thankful she wasn't another stage-struck young girl looking for an easy road to fame. He was thankful for her cool efficiency, too, and told her so often. When she had asked to take her two weeks vacation a little early, he had not been happy about it, but he had given his consent. He hadn't wanted to see her go. But he would survive with temporary help, he told her, and she knew any girl who replaced her would find him patient and fair. For Amanda, the best part of it was that he was happily married and was friendly with her in a way that never went beyond the boundaries of platonic good will. She had looked for that, wanted it desperately after Colin.

She had fallen in love with Colin from almost the first day she went to work for him, and those weeks before he began to take her out had been bittersweet. The next year had been one of the happiest of her life—and it had brought her to the unhappiest. Colin had never really loved her, she knew that now. She had dated him for a year before he had asked her to be his wife. And even after they were engaged, his kisses had been tender rather than passionate. He had never tried to make love to her. She had thought his lack of passion was a sign of respect for her and an unwillingness to disturb the tranquility of their working rapport. But after he met Lisa, he had broken off their engagement with a ruthless speed that left Amanda reeling. The cool lawyer who considered every angle vanished, to be replaced by a man who didn't bother to hide his eagerness to leave the office for a luncheon date with Lisa, and who lingered over his telephone calls with her, knowing a client waited impatiently in the outer office to see him. It was so out of character for Colin that Amanda had remained at her job for a few days after his engagement, getting up and going to work hollow-eyed after a night of restless tossing, certain that Colin would descend from his hazy dreamworld to discover that he still loved her. They had shared so much. How could he throw it away so quickly, so carelessly?

But he could and did. After he announced his engagement to Lisa at a huge party, she could take no more. She gave him a day's notice and fled, booking a seat on a plane to New York the next day. And when she climbed into the plane that foggy morning, a cold numbness claimed her. She welcomed it. After days of searing pain, it was a relief to feel nothing at all. She developed a shell, a cocoon that protected her. Paradoxically, the men she met in New York found it and her intriguing. Her air of cool dignity was a challenge. She had never intended to become a recluse, and she hadn't. She dated several men, but as soon as she made it clear she had no intention of ending the night in the bedroom, they lost interest. One of them, though, had owned a stable outside Manhattan and had introduced her to riding. Tom Caulfield was an expert horseman and a good judge of people, too, as it turned out. He had led a dark, coppery bay out of the stables, a slightly more spirited animal than he usually gave beginners, and Amanda had loved the horse at first sight. The horse, too, seemed to know this was a gifted rider, for it wheeled and turned expertly under her hands. Tom told her she was a natural. She had grown to love the sport, and the horses, too, if she had told the truth. She loved everything about them, their soft brown eyes, the muscles that moved like silk under the smooth skin, their power, and their gentleness. Even after she was no longer seeing Tom, she shopped carefully, spent little on food, and moved into a crowded apartment with three other girls in order to have the money for her riding fees. She rode on weekends and holidays, loving the wild freedom of flying through the air on the back of a horse. It was her one passion.

The warmth of the sun washed over her, and she realized this was the first time she had relaxed in almost twenty-four hours. Her eyelids felt like lead weights; she knew she should open them and watch for Buchanan, but she couldn't. The red-gold lashes lay against her cheeks and the sun turned her hair to fire, and she dozed. Then the sun went under a cloud and a chill touched her. She moved slightly, trying to get the sun to come back. Her eyes opened and she stared at a pair of black shoes and light-gray trousers directly in front of her.

Up past a length of muscular leg, past a casually open jacket, past a white shirt and gray silk tie her eyes traveled to collide with the slightly amused smile on the face of Reid Buchanan.

35

She straightened in the chair and ran her hand over her hair in an instinctive gesture. "Have you been standing there long?" she asked, angry all over again that he should have caught her dozing.

"Not long," he said calmly.

"Well, why didn't you say something?" she said waspishly. "You surely can't waste your precious time standing about watching people sleep." She stood up, straining to gain what little edge her height would have next to his.

He was smiling at her lazily, rather like a father at his little daughter. But his next words were anything but fatherly. "It rather depends on the people. I can't remember when I've watched a woman as beautiful as you asleep."

"Then you must certainly broaden your range, Mr. Buchanan."

He laughed openly at her, his teeth white in a tanned face.

"You find that amusing?" she asked, her voice razor-sharp.

"I find you amusing," he said, his voice still warm with humor. "You're like a child that's been roused from its nap too soon. Were you as bad-tempered then as you are now?"

Her color deepened. "You may find this hard to believe, but out of your presence I'm rarely angry."

He took her elbow and guided her toward the elevator. "Do I disturb your equilibrium that much, Miss Kirk?"

She was silent, trying to deal with the double onslaught of clamoring nerve ends in her arm and the disturbing knowledge that he did indeed have the power to arouse her emotions as no one had since Colin.

"Well, never mind," he said complacently as the doors

opened and he gave her a gentle push forward. "Perhaps you'll be better-tempered after you've eaten."

She opened her mouth to protest, but she saw the lift of his eyebrow out of the corner of her eyes as he anticipated her sharp retort. She clamped her lips together. His smile flashed again as she turned around and was forced to stand closer to him while other people boarded the elevator.

Even in the quiet elegance of the Top of the Mark, people noticed Reid Buchanan as they were shown to their table by a window. It was that air of command, she thought, combined with a virility that was all the more powerful because he seemed unaware of it. It was his air of command, too, she was sure, that earned them a table set for two next to the window with the most glorious view of the city. The Hood Mansion and the bridge were a part of it, along with the Fairmont Tower across the street.

She tried to regain her composure as she took off her coat and settled into the chair, but the sunny room, the white cloth-covered tables, and the tasteful music brought back so sharply the many times she had lunched here with Colin that she was driven to say what she had to say and leave Reid Buchanan to eat his lunch alone. She leaned toward him and said, "Mr. Buchanan, I—"

Silvery eyes flickered over her. "I never discuss anything before a meal, Miss Kirk. I find people are much too irritable." His smile mocked her and left her in little doubt as to just which one of them was irritated. A steward appeared with a wine list, but Reid waved it away saying, "I'd like a glass of Burgundy for the lady, and I'll have a dry Chablis."

Wine and women. How well he knew them. She caught

the steward's eye and said coolly, "Nothing for me, please."

The steward, plainly distressed, shot a look at Reid Buchanan.

"Bring what I've ordered. If the lady chooses not to drink it, that's her privilege," he said calmly.

The steward nodded with relief. "Very good, sir."

"This isn't a social outing," she said. "We're here to talk about—"

"Miss Kirk," he said, leaning back in his chair with a lazy grace. "Do you want something from me?"

Caught, she said, "I . . . I came to ask your assistance—"

"Then you'll sit back and relax and pretend to enjoy yourself. You have pretended civility in male company once or twice in your life, haven't you?" He smiled, but there was steel in his voice.

"Why should I?" she shot back, annoyed. "You haven't been particularly polite to me."

"But then I'm not going to *ask* you for anything, am I?" came the cool reply. She sat back, gritting her teeth, knowing she couldn't argue with his logic.

The steward appeared with the glasses of sparkling liquid and set the red one in front of Amanda and the clear wine at Reid's place.

Buchanan lifted his own in a silent salute and his eyes glinted at her from over the rim of the glass. She made no move to pick up her goblet. With a lift of an eyebrow, he sipped his wine and set the glass down. "I find your determination to remain sober quite flattering, Miss Kirk. Are you really that afraid of me?"

With a quick movement, she reached for her glass and lifted it to her lips. It was cool and heavy with the sweet-

38

ness of grapes ripened on a sunny hillside. She returned the glass to the table and stared at him with green eyes that matched the wine's sparkle.

His own were lazily amused. His mouth quirked as the steward came to take their orders and she announced that she wanted her meal put on a separate check. There was another silence as the young man glanced at Reid, who merely moved his shoulders dismissively under the smooth material of his jacket.

The steward turned to Amanda and, nodding, took her order for the sole amandine. Reid Buchanan also chose the fish. When he folded the menu and handed it back, he turned to Amanda. "Where are you working at the present time?"

She reached forward to touch the stem of her glass with her slender fingers. "I'm a secretary for a theatrical agent in New York City," she said coolly.

"What does a theatrical agent do?" One dark brow lifted as if he couldn't believe a theatrical agent did anything of real value.

"He matches people with jobs. Television producers contact him for leads on people, people contact him for leads on jobs in the theater or in TV series."

"While you type out contracts, answer the telephone, and promise not to accept any roles as the leading lady."

"There's no question of that," she retorted. "I'm no actress."

"No," he said blandly. "I've already noticed that."

Hot, aromatic fish surrounded by bright carrots and green peas was placed in front of her. Amanda suddenly realized how little she had had to eat in the last several hours.

"But you're a native of San Francisco," Reid said, continuing to probe the corners of her private life after the waiter had left them.

She wanted to tell him it was none of his business, but she was determined to match his casual air. "Yes," she said, forking the delicate fish tantalizing her nose. "My father is head of a construction company here."

"Kirk Construction Company," he murmured, something flickering in his eyes.

"Yes. You've heard of it?"

"Only in passing," he said casually. "How long have you been in New York?"

"A year." She brought the napkin up to her lips. His eyes glanced over her slender fingers. She laid the napkin quickly back in her lap.

"And in that time," he said, his mouth curving in a smile, "you've gotten neither engaged nor married."

She looked directly at his lean, dark face. "My personal life is not your concern," she said.

"It could be." The words were softly suggestive.

She had expected it, but somehow the easy assumption that she would respond to a casual pass infuriated her. "It couldn't," she said flatly.

He watched her sit back and lay her fork quite deliberately on her plate as if she had lost her appetite, his eyes amused. "I like to know the people I'm dealing with," he said.

"You're not dealing with me, Mr. Buchanan," she said coldly.

"Quite the contrary, Miss Kirk." He contradicted her smoothly, easily, as if she were a recalcitrant member of the board. "You've taken up more of my time today than I normally give any one person during a twenty-four-hour period."

40

"I'm sorry," she said, her voice low and intense. "I didn't ask for this much time. You were the one who insisted on lunch."

"All right," he said, leaning back in his chair as if he were tired of baiting her. "Suppose you tell me what your problem is . . . with David." His eyes were lazily hooded, but Amanda knew that behind his bland expression, he was watching her with hawklike scrutiny.

"I came to talk to you about your brother and—" Her voice failed her.

"Yes," he prompted, waiting.

She took a breath. "He and my sister—"

"Your sister," he murmured. "I might have guessed."

She didn't ask how he might have guessed. "There's a possibility they might . . . might decide to run away and get married," she finished in a rush. He frowned, and she plunged into speech again, anxious for him to understand that she did not approve. "My father is not pleased, and I . . . I understand your mother isn't well, and that she hasn't met Susan."

"No," he agreed, his face revealing no emotion, "she hasn't."

She faced him squarely and continued. "If Susan and David could be persuaded to wait a little longer, if they had your . . . your blessing, it might prevent them from acting hastily now."

"You mean," he stated coolly, "you want me to tell David to wait?"

Amanda took a breath. "I know you're opposed to the whole idea of your brother marrying. But if you could give your qualified consent to, say, marriage in another year, after Susan began college, we might gain enough time to allow your mother and my father to become accustomed

41

to the idea. And if it is nothing but a youthful infatuation, which is entirely possible, it will die of its own accord."

"And that's what you hope will happen," he said, his eyes cool.

"I have no feeling about it at all. If Susan truly loves David and he loves her, that love will sustain them through a year."

He studied her, his face enigmatic. "And you want me to participate in this . . . this programmed plan to marriage?"

It was the hostile response she had expected. "I thought it was at least a reasonable compromise. Otherwise—" She didn't finish, leaving him to imagine what he would, a hasty marriage in some Mexican village.

"And suppose," he drawled, "that during this year of their engagement Susan and David anticipate their marriage vows, and your sister finds she is carrying David's child? How do you think my mother—and your father—would feel about that? Even in this day of relaxed moral values, my mother would find it extremely distasteful to have her first grandchild born too soon after a hole-in-the-corner affair of a wedding."

It was something she hadn't thought about. She stared at him, a red flush staining her cheeks. "Do you want me to assure you that my sister is a perfect saint who would never allow such a thing to happen? Well, I can't!" she said clearly. "My sister is a young girl who loves your brother very much, or thinks she does. What you've suggested is a distinct possibility. And if you think you've insulted my sister, you're wrong. It's natural for a girl to want to give herself to a man she loves very much."

His eyes met hers with no embarrassment. "It never occurred to me that I was insulting your sister. I was merely pointing out some salient facts of the situation, Miss Kirk. I've learned to my regret that when you're dealing with the odd species known as Homo sapiens, you have to consider every facet of the situation."

"Susan and David are both of age," Amanda stated coldly. "There's no way anyone could monitor every minute of their time together—"

"I wasn't suggesting anyone should. I'm saying that rather than preventing or delaying their marriage, we should do everything in our power to accomplish their legal union with all possible speed."

He sat there looking at her calmly as if he hadn't just done the most astounding volte-face she had ever experienced. She sat still, sure that her brain had not interpreted his words correctly. "You mean," she said at last, "let them marry right away?"

"As I understand the situation, Miss Kirk, as you've presented it to me, it isn't a matter of *letting them do anything*. It's merely a matter of lending them our approval or not. And as you've rightly said, it would be much better if they married with both their families' knowledge and approval." He paused and looked at her. "So if you're asking my opinion, I think we should do everything in our power to expedite their marriage."

"Expedite it!" She exploded. "You make it sound like"— she struggled for the words—"like a business merger!"

"Are you accusing me of being less than romantic?" he asked, his mouth turning up at the corners. "I could hardly be less so than you—"

"Amanda! It is you! I thought I was seeing things."

She didn't need Reid Buchanan to shift his gaze to the point behind her shoulder and say "Hello, Brent," to know that Colin was standing next to their table. It had been bound to happen; she supposed in a way she had been waiting for it, at least she had been until Reid Buchanan had forced her to focus all her attention on him. Now she turned and looked into the handsome face and brilliant blue eyes that had haunted her dreams for a year. Next to him stood a woman, a tiny, glossy thing dressed in a red suit with dark hair pulled into an intricate French twist. Amanda had seen many pictures of Lisa Wallingford, but she had never met her. Of course, she was Lisa Brent now.

Amanda clasped her hands in her lap and raised her head, fighting the sensation that she was an overly large specimen of womanhood next to a lovely doll. "Hello, Colin," she said. "How are you?" Her voice sounded cool and normal enough, but her face felt as if it were on fire. She saw Colin's eyes move speculatively from her to Buchanan.

He said, "I didn't know you knew Amanda, Reid."

"We were just getting acquainted," he stated calmly.

"In fact, Amanda, I didn't know you were back in town," Colin said. "Your father told me you flew away to the Big Apple."

She was conscious of Reid's eyes on her as she said, "Yes, I found a job in New York."

"Aren't you going to introduce me, darling?" Lisa Brent asked, plainly disturbed that another woman had garnered so much attention while she was forced to stand quietly on the sidelines.

Colin seemed to be staring at Amanda and not hearing his wife. "I just can't believe it." Lisa gave him a nudge with her elbow and he said, "Oh—I'm sorry, darling," automatically, as if he said it often. "This is Amanda Kirk. Lisa Brent, my wife."

Try as she might, she found no trace of hesitation or

self-consciousness in his introduction of his ex-fiancée to his wife.

"Hello," Lisa said, her voice pitched seductively low. Her eyes, which had been bright for Colin and Reid, were something less than that for Amanda. "I haven't heard Colin speak of you before."

"No, I'm sure you haven't," Amanda said coolly. "I was his secretary for several years, but I left him shortly after he became engaged to you."

"You must have been in love with your boss," she said, coyly clinging to Colin's arm, her long red nails bright against the dark blue of his suit jacket.

"Perhaps I was . . . a little," Amanda said coolly, her eyes on Colin's face. "But I got over it," she finished lightly.

"Darling, you didn't tell me you had an old flame hanging about San Francisco. It must have slipped your mind."

Colin's face hardened. "Amanda was a good secretary, and a good friend."

That hurt more than she thought it possibly could.

"And now your old flame is lunching with my old flame," Lisa said with a malicious little laugh. "That's a joke on us, isn't it, darling?"

"Yes, isn't it?"

There was something cold and unpleasant in Colin's clipped words. Amanda had never heard him use that tone of voice to anyone before. Colin stared down into Lisa's upturned face with a hard line around his mouth that told Amanda he was angry. Was Lisa involved with Reid Buchanan? Knowing his reputation, it was all too likely. But whatever her faults, Colin loved Lisa, of that Amanda was sure. Amanda had never seen Colin become angry with her during their entire year of courtship, and she realized now it was because she had never really aroused any strong emotion in him. He had found her a pleasant companion—*a good friend*—and he liked having her around, but he had never felt the consuming passion for her he still seemed to feel for Lisa.

Lisa laughed, a low, husky sound. How could such a low voice come from such a small body? "You know me, darling. I see humor in the strangest situations." She laughed again, and Colin paled, his mouth tighter than before. Then she said, "Reid, we haven't seen you in positively ages. I was so disappointed that you weren't able to attend our housewarming. But I understood why when I saw your picture in the paper the next day with that gorgeous actress. Why don't you bring her with you and come for dinner tomorrow night?"

"I'm sorry, that's not possible, Lisa," Reid Buchanan declined politely. "I'm leaving the country this afternoon."

She made a pouting mouth of regret and then brightened. "But you must come next week. I'm having a party —"

Reid Buchanan shook his head. "You know I can't promise anything that far ahead, Lisa. I never know what my schedule will be. If I have the evening free, I might look in for a while."

"Don't you forget then, darling. I'm dying to have you see our house."

"I won't forget," Reid assured her.

She walked away without a backward glance at Amanda. Colin watched her go with an exasperated look and then said, "I'll call you, Amanda." She nodded, but he had already turned away to follow Lisa to their table across the room. Amanda watched him seat his wife in a chair. There was nothing inside her but a strange, empty feeling.

"So you were in love with Colin Brent," a low voice said, and Amanda returned her attention to the man across the table from her.

"It wasn't a secretary's crush-on-the-boss thing," she said, wanting him to know the truth for some reason she couldn't explain. "We were engaged for a year." She looked up into that dark face and saw the sardonic lift of his lips. "It's over," she said, gesturing helplessly in the general direction they had gone. "You can see that. We parted friends."

"Did you?" His silver-gray eyes watched her, almost as if he were analyzing her every reaction and feeding it through the computer of his mind. "Is that possible?"

"You saw." Her hand trembled and in an effort to control her jumbled emotions she clung to the stem of her wineglass. Her grip made the wine undulate in the glass. Over half of it remained.

"He lunches here quite regularly, doesn't he?" He didn't seem to require an answer. "Is that the reason you didn't want to come here with me?" he guessed astutely.

She neither confirmed nor denied his statement but made a convulsive movement with her hand, an abortive attempt to lift the wineglass to her lips. Her fatigue and the jarring encounter with Colin and his wife had thrown off her reactions. She caught the foot of the glass under the rim of her plate and spilled the wine into it and onto her lap. The red liquid spread over the beige fabric of her dress with unbelievable speed and thoroughness. She felt as if she had been branded.

"Oh!" she cried out in distress. Reid Buchanan was on his feet at once.

47

"What the—" He surveyed the damage with a grim mouth. Amanda daubed at her dress with her napkin, feeling like an utter fool. Reid lifted his hand. A steward appeared instantly at his elbow. Reid drew a bill from his pocket and took Amanda's coat from the back of her chair. "Settle the bill for me, please. I'm going to see Miss Kirk to my suite."

"That isn't necessary," Amanda protested, rising. "My coat will cover it—" Reid was already helping her into it and standing protectively in front of her so that no one in the dining room could see the results of her clumsiness. "I'll call a cab," she finished lamely.

"Don't be an idiot," he said sharply. "Your dress will be ruined if the wine isn't removed immediately. One of the hotel staff can take care of it for you."

"No." Amanda kept her voice low, but even as she spoke, he was guiding her through the dining room and into the hallway. They were at the elevator. "I'm not going with you."

He turned cool eyes on her. "Then I'll have to buy you a dress to replace that one."

"You'll do nothing of the kind."

"If I hadn't ordered the wine, you wouldn't have spilled it," he said.

"You're not to blame," she said huskily, but the elevator arrived and she was propelled into it by the iron hand on her elbow.

"Perhaps not," he agreed, "but I feel responsible."

She leaned back against the cool chrome-bar support and stared at the implacable line of his jaw. The door had closed and the elevator was moving down. It would have been easier to swim away from a riptide. His calm air of command defeated her.

Why was he taking so much time with her? He had said he was leaving for Madrid. He was a man who didn't believe in wasting a moment, she knew that. Mute evidence of his organization was the oxblood overnight case and matching shaving kit propped on top, packed and ready, sitting on the cream-colored rug just inside the door.

He walked her through the spacious lounge with the same firm hand. She caught a glimpse of dark antique furniture and a wide window that no doubt commanded a view as expansive as the one they had just left. His bedroom was done in cream and bronze. Something of his personality was in the air, an excitement, a quickening of the blood. It said something about the impact of a man when even a hotel room sang with the essence of him. She averted her eyes from the king-sized bed covered with a cream-print silk coverlet.

He guided her into the bathroom. "Take your dress off," he said as if he were discussing the weather. "You can wear my robe. It's here."

He closed the door and left her there in a gold-fauceted, mirror-tiled wonder of a bathroom that looked like something in the movies. There was no other outlet than to do as she had been told.

She took off her coat and stripped out of the wine-soaked dress. His robe, a soft gray full-length velour with a hood, hung behind the door. Lined in black, it enveloped her. She looked like a monk in it, she thought wryly as she saw herself in the mirror.

Reid Buchanan might look like a monk in it, too, but he was far from being one, she surmised as she noticed the bottles of cosmetics lined along the glass shelf under the mirror, ready for use. My Sin, how appropriate. Arpège,

49

a facial cleanser, and an overnight cream. Were these kept in readiness for Lisa? Was he her lover? The thought brought a violent shudder of distaste.

A knock on the door was followed by the immediate sound of it opening, and she turned, a sharp word of protest on her lips. A woman in a black uniform stood there, a gray-haired woman with light blue eyes that shone at her.

"Mr. Buchanan says you've had an accident, lovey," she said, picking Amanda's dress up off the counter. She clucked sympathetically when she saw the dark stain. "You did have a bit of trouble, didn't you? Well, never mind," she said comfortingly. "We'll have it right as rain for you in no time at all."

She turned and walked through the open doorway, not bothering to close the door. Amanda was left standing in full view of the bedroom, and Reid Buchanan.

His eyes moved leisurely over her, as if he enjoyed her discomfort. The disconcerting smell of expensive male cologne drifted from the folds of his robe as she stepped out of the bathroom, hoping to ease the sense of intimacy. But as she started to walk toward him, his eyes glittered with amusement, and she halted. There was a silence in the room as he studied her slender body clothed in his lounging garment. Then he said, "We haven't finished our discussion. Will you come through to the lounge, or did you want to continue it here?" His eyes gleamed at her as he saw her consciously avert her eyes from the bed.

"No, of course not," she said shortly, picking up the long length of robe so that she wouldn't trip and walked by him to the comparative safety of the lounge.

But it didn't feel any safer there. She was as supremely conscious of him behind her as she had been in the bedroom. She avoided sitting down on the couch. She went to stand in front of the window, pretending an interest in the view. He continued across the room to a narrow table that held several bottles of expensive liquors. "Would you care for a drink?"

She shook her head. "I think I've had enough for one day. And I . . . I'm sure you must be in a hurry—"

"I have a few minutes yet." He poured himself a portion of what looked like Scotch, but he didn't drink it. He held the glass in his hand, turning it idly. He seemed to be watching the play of light on the surface of the amber liquid. Then his eyes lifted to her. "Does your sister have hair like yours?"

She was strangely disturbed by the question. "It's red, yes, but slightly darker, more auburn than mine. Why?"

"I was just"—his voice seemed low and husky—"wondering if I should look forward to having a red-haired niece or nephew."

Turbulent emotion washed through her. She thrust her hands into the pockets of his robe, clenching them together to ease the tightening nerves in her stomach. "I would hope they would wait to have children."

"Your mother died some years ago, if I remember correctly."

Amanda nodded. "She had leukemia. She died when I was thirteen and Susan was six."

"You were . . . Susan's mother after that."

Amanda hesitated and then said, "I suppose you could say that. We had a woman in to clean, and Benita, Dad's secretary, took us to dentist appointments. But, yes, I watched out for Susan. I was old enough."

"How old is your sister now?"

"Eighteen."

51

"That makes you twenty-five."

She lifted an eyebrow. "You thought I was older."

He smiled. "Did I?"

She made an impatient move with her shoulders. "Most people do. I suppose it was a maturing experience, losing my mother, being responsible—"

"Yet you fell in love with Colin Brent . . . unwisely."

A slow flush rose in her cheeks, and she clenched her hands until her nails bit into the palms. She could guess what he was leading up to—and none too subtly either. "What I did or didn't do has nothing to do with Susan and David. It's them we're supposed to be discussing, not me."

"But your own unhappy experience explains your ambiguous feelings about Susan and David—"

Goaded at last to the point of no return, she flared. "My ambiguous feelings! What about your own, Mr. Buchanan? As I understand it, you flatly refused to meet Susan last Christmas and told David he was too young to think of getting married and that he should be seeing other women."

"The very fact that he didn't listen to me indicates the depth of his feeling for your sister," Reid Buchanan returned implacably. "I'm able to accept that as a sign that his love for Susan is genuine. I knew it the moment you told me they were still seeing each other. David has never dated a girl longer than two months or so before. Sometimes he's dated several at one time. Granted, I didn't listen to him at Christmas because I was judging him on his past performance. But the fact remains that he *has* proposed marriage to Susan and has even considered eloping with her. I know my brother well enough to know when he is serious and not let my own experiences with the opposite sex cloud my judgment about him. Can you say the same, Miss Kirk? Do you know your sister as well?" Then he added softly, "Or yourself so little?"

It was ridiculous, she knew, to attempt a dignified yet affronted appearance as she straightened in that robe with its velvet lining touching her skin as sensuously as the fur of a kitten and her every curve clearly outlined. Yet she tried. "I came to see you because I wanted to clear away misunderstandings, not add to them. If I've convinced you that David is sincere about Susan, I'm glad. But I assure you, I'll do my best not to let any personal qualms I might have spoil Susan's happiness."

"Good," he said, clipping the word and turning away from the table as if he'd just accomplished a satisfactory business transaction. "Then you'll have no objection to coming with us next weekend to visit my mother."

He turned his back to deposit the glass on the table and she stood stunned, staring with a sense of dismay at the smooth cloth that spanned those wide shoulders. She had been neatly and cleverly maneuvered into a corner. But he would not find her so easily pushed about. "Why should I?" she countered coolly. "Susan doesn't need a chaperone."

He turned back, a smile touching his lips. "You've admitted that you practically raised the girl. My mother will expect to meet you, Susan's surrogate mother. Jane can't travel, a trip to San Francisco is out of the question for her. Merely out of common courtesy to her, you should come."

"No, I'm sorry," Amanda said, shaking her head, shutting out his infallible logic. "It's out of the question. I came to spend time with my father—"

"He's invited too, of course," Reid Buchanan countered smoothly.

53

Amanda shook her head. "I can't speak for my father—I don't know what his plans are—but—"

"You have a week to clear your schedule," he said coolly. "My mother will be expecting you." Then, after neatly boxing her in, he added, "I'll be back a week from today. We'll fly up to the ranch in my plane."

"I really don't think—"

"Consider the pleasure you'll be giving my mother. She's always wanted girls around the house." He paused, then said, "Have you ever been on a working ranch?"

"No, but . . . I wouldn't want to think that we were inconveniencing your mother in any way—"

"You won't be," he said shortly, striding to the table next to his cases and pulling a bill from his pocket to throw on the smooth surface. "Give Mrs. MacCrea my thanks and tell her that's for her. I'll contact you next week."

He picked up his cases and let himself out of the suite, closing the door quietly behind him. Amanda stared after him in dismay. She had even given him a tentative yes. Such was the skill and expertise of Reid Buchanan when it came to getting what he wanted. She remembered Susan saying something to that effect. But why did he want her to go? Was it just for the sake of his mother? Something told her not to look at any other thought too closely. The thought of spending an entire weekend in his disturbing company was a sobering one. What should she do? She didn't have to go, and yet . . . where did her obligations lie? She had begun this, she could at least see it through.

She pondered her dilemma even as the woman returned with her dress. Amanda told her about the bill and watched her slip it into her pocket and nod as she went out the door. She felt no better as she took off Reid Buchanan's robe and hung it on a hook on the door. As she

dressed, combed her hair, put on her coat, and walked out
the door of the suite, she knew Reid Buchanan was right
about one thing. She didn't seem to know herself at all.
She had thought she was immune to any man. But there
was only one thing that could make her so apprehensive
about spending a weekend on his mother's ranch. And
that was Reid Buchanan's own dark attraction, she realized with a little shock as she stepped into the elevator.

CHAPTER 3

A sober-eyed Susan answered her ring at the apartment door. "Where on earth have you been?" she burst out as she stepped back to allow Amanda to come inside. "I've been out of my mind. I thought the earth had swallowed you up."

"I'm sorry," Amanda said, taking off her coat and running a hand through the red-gold strands of her long hair. "I should have called you." She dropped her coat over the back of the couch and said, "Let's go into the kitchen, shall we? I could use a cup of tea."

Susan studied her for a long moment and then turned to lead the way to the small alcove that was the kitchen. "Sit there," she said, pointing to the snack bar that jutted into the middle of the room like a peninsula. "I'll put the kettle on. I've been positively dying to hear what happened. Did you get to see him?"

"We had lunch together. I—"

Susan turned from the stove to stare at Amanda, her eyes wide. "He took you to lunch?"

"Not exactly. It was the only time he could see me." Susan turned back to fill the kettle with water. Amanda was relieved to be away from the discerning gaze of her sister's sharp eyes. Quickly, she said, "I told him about you and David. Then . . . I suggested that the two of you might wait a year if you were sure of his blessing. That was my own idea, darling. I thought it would be better for you, and more acceptable to him."

"You did?" Susan said, placing the kettle on the stove with a thump as if she didn't agree.

"Yes, I did. But it wasn't."

"I knew it," Susan said flatly. "I knew he wouldn't agree to our marriage under any condition."

"No." Amanda shook her head. "You're wrong. He didn't agree to a year waiting period because . . . because he thinks it would be better if you married immediately."

Susan sat down on the high stool across from Amanda as if her legs had suddenly failed to hold her up. "Immediately! I don't believe it!"

"I didn't quite believe it, either," Amanda said huskily. "But he's offered us all an invitation to meet his mother at her ranch next weekend, and I hardly think he would do so if he wasn't serious about it."

"But, Amanda, it doesn't make any sense," Susan argued, frowning with perplexity. "Why has he changed his mind?"

There was no need to tell Susan that Reid Buchanan thought she might have a child before time, no need at all. If Susan were going to become a Buchanan, it would be infinitely better if her marriage started with an easing of tension between herself and David's brother rather than the reverse. Carefully, Amanda said, "He pointed out that if you're planning on eloping, his permission or anyone else's isn't necessary. You and David are of age. He feels it would be much better for everyone concerned if you married with both your families' blessings as soon as possible."

57

"I still don't believe it," Susan said, shaking her head. The kettle began to whistle as if to punctuate her bewilderment. She rose and reached to pour the steaming water into the teapot. "What kind of magic did you work on him?"

Amanda moved slightly on the stool, thinking of what little effect she had had on him and what great impact he had had on her. "I didn't do anything. That's his honest opinion. But if you must know, I don't agree. I don't think you should rush into marriage just because he's condoning it. He's hardly a qualified judge," she said. "You need time to see if your feeling for David is real and not something that will die away in the boredom of everyday living."

Susan poured the tea into Amanda's cup and set it in front of her. "I'm never bored when I'm with David," she said emphatically. "He's the only thing that has kept me sane this last year."

"But people change," Amanda insisted, her face mobile with concern. "You're young. You'll change, David will change."

"But that's just it, Amanda," Susan said passionately, her eyes glowing. "If we're married, we'll change together. We'll learn when we have to tiptoe around each other, and when each of us needs to be alone, and when we need to be together." A tender look softened her young face.

"But what about your school, your art work?"

"Don't you see, Amanda? That's one career I can pursue at home. We've already decided I'd go to school even after we're married. We had planned to get an apartment close to the Institute. David will continue to work for Western. It will be ideal. Oh, Amanda"—her eyes sparkled—"I can't thank you enough for going to see David's brother. You've made everything *wonderful!*"

Amanda's fingers tightened on her cup. "But . . . suppose you have a child."

"I hope we do," Susan said indomitably. "Right away. The baby will be an excellent model for my drawing."

Amanda rubbed her temple with one slender hand.

"You know why you dislike the idea of my getting married, don't you?" Susan's eyes were clear.

Amanda returned her direct look. "I'm not opposed to it in principle, Susan. I just think you should wait."

"David is nothing like Colin," Susan said flatly.

"I never suggested he was," Amanda replied.

"I—don't let's say things to each other like this, Amanda. It's just that I want you to be as happy for me as I am," she said earnestly. "Forget about Colin." She lifted her eyebrows. "He deserves Lisa. She suits him exactly. Her father is rich and influential, not like . . . well, anyway, I think you had a lucky escape," she finished, her voice raised slightly with her conviction. "Amanda, you were blind to his faults because you were infatuated with him. But he was a phony. He divided the world into four parts." She ticked them off on her fingers. "One, intelligent and rich; two, important and rich; three, stupid and rich; four, none of the above and not worth bothering about." Susan stopped to catch her breath. "David's not like that. He's been around the world, traveling for Western. He's met people, all kinds of people. He knows people have faults, but that they have good points, too. He's tolerant. He knows what he wants out of life. He doesn't want to live in a hotel suite and constantly be packing a suitcase like his brother does. He wants a home and a wife. And he wants me to be that wife. And that's what I want too, Amanda. I love him very much."

She stared at Amanda for a long moment. Then, suddenly embarrassed by her impassioned speech, she looked down at her cup. Amanda studied the glossy bent head. Then she said, "If that's what you want, I . . . wish you all the happiness in the world."

Susan leaned forward impulsively and touched her hand. "I want you to be happy too, Amanda. You've got to forget the unhappiness Colin caused you. You don't want to end up living alone all your life because the first man you ever tried to love was a complete idiot, do you?"

Amanda had to smile. "I've gotten over him, darling," she said calmly. "I . . . I saw him today at the Mark, and it was like . . . like seeing a stranger."

"Good, I'm glad," Susan said stoutly. "Was his wife with him?"

"Yes," Amanda said, and then added, "she's very beautiful."

Susan made a sound in her throat. "If you like stuck-up snobs. I met her once at a party." Susan launched into a full description of the party she had been invited to at one of the houses on the bay. Amanda tried to focus her attention, but suddenly fatigue made her body sag. She felt weary and drained.

Susan stopped in midsentence. "Amanda, I'm sorry. Here I am, running on, and you must be exhausted. Go lie down. I'll go out and get something for dinner."

Amanda made an attempt to protest, but Susan was adamant. Almost before she realized it, Susan had her in the bedroom, had helped her out of her dress, and was tucking her between the scented sheets of the single bed across from Susan's. The thought drifted across her mind that Susan had relished the role reversal. And there, in that dark limbo before sleep overtook her, she seemed to see the sun glint off the wings of a silver plane, a plane that circled the sunny skies of Spain.

Amanda woke in the morning refreshed. She had slept through the dinner hour, through Susan's slipping into the bed across from her. Susan told her that her father had already left for the office. Amanda regretted her sleepiness. She had wanted to talk to him about Reid Buchanan's invitation.

She and Susan shopped in the Victorian section of Cow Hollow that afternoon and rode the cable car home, clinging to the side laughing. When Maxwell Kirk did arrive at the apartment late that afternoon, he looked tired and drawn. Amanda had to hold her tongue. They ate together, and he retired to his room at once. On Sunday, he was gone again before Amanda got up.

When the same thing occurred on Monday morning, Amanda asked Susan, "I don't believe this. How long has it been going on?"

They sat in the kitchen in robes and slippers, drinking their morning coffee. "Almost a month." Susan's eyes were guarded.

"Why—" The phone rang in the living room. A look of relief passed over Susan's face. "Excuse me," she said and walked into the other room, leaving Amanda to worry alone in the kitchen. Why was her father driving himself to the point of exhaustion? And why was Susan unwilling to talk about it?

She heard her sister's low tones, but she couldn't understand anything that was said. When Susan returned, Amanda asked, "Was it David?"

Susan shook her head, averting her eyes. "It was Benita."

"Benita? Why would she call here on a Monday morning?" Amanda asked.

Susan's eyes skittered away from Amanda's. "Benita isn't Dad's secretary anymore, Amanda. He let her go a couple of weeks ago."

Amanda stared at her sister. "Let her go!" she exclaimed. "Why would he do that? She knows as much about that business as he does. He'll be helpless without her! He never could file anything correctly, and I don't think he's ever once composed an answer to a letter himself. He just tossed everything to her and said, 'Take care of this, you know what to say.'"

"I know that." Susan sat quietly, stirring her coffee.

"Susan, something is wrong. And whatever it is, I think you'd better tell me about it. Now."

Susan raised reluctant eyes to Amanda. "Dad didn't want you to know because he knew how fond you were of Benita." She sighed. "He hasn't said anything to me, but I'm almost sure he's in financial trouble."

She had been a fool, Amanda thought miserably. She should have guessed. There had been enough signs: his physical appearance, his plea for her to deal with the problem of Susan, his long hours at the office. Dismissing Benita was the definitive clue.

"How bad is it?"

Susan shook her head. "I have no idea. You know Dad. He carries his troubles by himself. You never know what he's thinking."

Amanda knew that was true. "Where's Benita working now?"

"A construction firm in Oakland. She didn't have any trouble finding another job. She keeps in touch." Susan looked up at Amanda from the swirling liquid in her cup.

"I think Benita's always been a little in love with Dad. She still worries about him. That's why she called this morning, to remind him about some luncheon he has at the end of the week where he should take a steno with him. She offered to drive over on her lunch hour and go."

"You mean he hasn't hired another secretary part time?"

Susan shook her head. "I hate to say this, Amanda, but I think he was torn between trying to keep his troubles to himself so you wouldn't know and hoping you'd come to the office and help him."

Amanda shook her head. "He hasn't said one word."

"You know he wouldn't. We're supposed to read his mind, I guess. But he must need you desperately, Amanda. Would you mind very much spending a few days of your vacation in another office?"

"No, of course not," she said, rising. "I'll go and get dressed."

It was like stepping back in time to get out of the taxi in front of the building on Montgomery Street, to walk into that ancient elevator and be lifted creakily to the sixth floor, and to enter that rabbit warren of filing cabinets and cracked leather chairs that was her father's office. Nothing had changed. The only addition seemed to be a thick coat of dust on Benita's philodendron, and the gray plastic cover on her typewriter. In all the years Amanda had run in and out of her father's domain, she could never remember seeing that typewriter covered.

She eased out of the green suit jacket she was wearing and metaphorically rolled up her sleeves, even though the sleeves of the amber silk blouse she wore were short and didn't require it. She dusted the philodendron with a rag she found in the bottom drawer of the desk and then sat down in Benita's chair—to her it would always be Benita's chair—and studied the piles of unopened mail scattered on the desk top. They were heaped roughly into five stacks, whether by day of arrival or by content she had no way of knowing. Her father's inner office door was closed, but she could hear his voice through the paneled door. He was speaking to someone on the telephone. The yellow light at the base of her own green phone was glowing.

She found a letter opener in the middle drawer of the desk. Reluctantly, she slid it under the flap of the first envelope. It was only by force of will that she continued on through the first pile of mail. When she had finished, she wished wholeheartedly she had never begun. If she had wanted any more proof of her father's financial woes, it was here, laid out in front of her in various degrees of cold demand.

Some were still polite. "It has come to our attention that—" Others did not spare words. "Remit immediately. Bill overdue." The last dozen or so warned bluntly that the bill had been turned over to a collection agency.

Amanda sat back, the chair creaking familiarly under her. She was appalled and shaken by the extent of her father's indebtedness. The agony of it was still in her eyes when her father emerged without warning from his office. He was halfway into the room before he saw her.

"Amanda!" He halted in front of her with shock in his eyes. One swift glance over the top of the desk told him she had become well acquainted with the state of his affairs in the last few minutes.

"I've had some setbacks," he began staunchly with a bravado that tore at her. When he saw the look of compassion in her eyes, he made a gesture of disgust with one

64

hand and sank into the chair in front of her desk. "What are you doing here, Amanda?" he asked, his face ashen. "I . . . I didn't want you involved in this." His hand swept over the desk.

"I'm here because I think you need me," she said quietly, aching to reassure him somehow.

His shoulders slumped. He ran one hand over his forehead. "There's nothing you can do. I'm not sure there's anything I can do."

"Isn't there a way to pay what you owe and start again?"

His eyes glittered with despair. "I had hoped . . . I wanted—" He thrust himself up out of the chair and began to pace in front of her. "I've got to have that renovation contract for the Art Museum. It's my only chance to get the company on its feet again. But I was talking to Colin just now, and he thinks Buchanan will be difficult. Some of the others on the committee are more amenable. I don't know exactly how Buchanan will stop me, but I'm sure if that's what he wants to do, he'll do it."

Amanda tried to ignore the shiver she felt at the sound of Reid Buchanan's name. "I thought you were doing well. The apartment, the car—"

"I've managed to live on the interest of the investments I made with the money I got from the sale of the house," he said, "but there's no question that I'm in a bad position financially. Buchanan knows about construction and what the market has been like the past few years. He knows I can't afford to fail, because of—" He stopped speaking.

Amanda said gently, "Because?"

He shook his head and turned his back to her. The grim look in his eyes made her reluctant to press him further for an answer.

Turning to her again, he urged Amanda to leave the office and enjoy her vacation. Only in the face of her flat refusal did he grudgingly give her permission to deal with the mail.

They established a procedure that first day. The rest of the week went by in much the same way. Amanda got up and rode to work with her father each morning, ate lunch at her desk with him, rode home with him at night. Her mind seemed to work on two levels every day, one part using her secretarial skills to help him prepare and present his bid to the committee on Friday, the other in a constant state of agonized worry about her father and the feeling he had been put on a long slide toward disaster.

On Friday, Amanda still had not told her father about Susan and her own invitation to the Buchanan ranch. She had been with her father enough to realize the name of Buchanan was anathema to him. Susan was home packing, ecstatic because she had received a call from David telling her they would be leaving the next morning. Amanda sat in front of the typewriter, wondering how she could broach the subject to her father. Everything depended on the success of his presentation at this luncheon meeting. She prayed that Colin had overestimated the antagonism of Reid Buchanan and that her father would sail through the presentation with no problems at all. But somehow she didn't really believe that. The image of Reid Buchanan, those silvery eyes that seemed to slice a person in two with just a look, remained in her mind. She was sure that if Buchanan had decided her father's company was not capable of doing the Museum renovation, he wouldn't hesitate to say so, even though he might be offending his brother's future father-in-law.

She resumed typing the letter she had been working on,

telling herself not to borrow trouble. *It hasn't been borrowed,* her mind whispered, *it's come to stay permanently.*

The morning crawled by. At eleven thirty, her father called her into his office. He stood behind his desk, shrugging into his suit jacket, putting his papers into his briefcase briskly. Fatigue and worry had caused his eyes to sink farther into his head. There was a nervous glitter in them as he said, "Well, Amanda, I'm ready." He snapped his briefcase shut. "Get your jacket."

Her heart began to hammer. "I'm to go with you?"

"I told Buchanan I was bringing my secretary, and you're my secretary, aren't you?"

"I really hadn't planned on—"

He gave her a wry smile. "I don't blame you. Go along then, take the rest of the day off. I'll see you at home."

The resolute set of his shoulders made her say, "Just a minute, Dad. I'm coming with you."

"I won't refuse," her father said ruefully. "I need all the support I can get."

It was only as they were getting into the car that she thought to ask, "Where is this meeting, Dad?"

He slid behind the wheel, a grim smile playing over his mouth. "On enemy territory, honey. Reid Buchanan's suite at the Mark Hopkins Hotel."

CHAPTER 4

She had heard of choosing to walk into the lion's den, but this was the first time she had actually done it. She doubted if any of the sophisticated people frequenting the lobby of the Mark thought about it as a lion's den, but she held no illusions about this luncheon. She had been on the receiving end of Reid Buchanan's incisive mind, and she knew it was not something one did for sheer enjoyment.

She linked her arm through her father's in a protective gesture. They crossed the marble floor and stepped into the elevator to be lifted to the fourteenth floor. As they walked down the hallway, Amanda's apprehension grew. The walls seemed close, her lungs protested. She swallowed once and smiled at her father. They were at the door waiting to be admitted when Maxwell Kirk's left hand went unconsciously to his tie to straighten the knot.

"You look fine, Dad," she said huskily. Her father smiled faintly.

The door was opened, and they were offered a drink from a tray carried by a white-jacketed waiter almost at once. Both Amanda and her father shook their heads, and the waiter nodded and walked away. Amanda stood with her back to the door, searching among the dozen men and women who stood around talking for the familiar dark head. Reid Buchanan was not there. The tension in Amanda released the hold it had on the muscles of her stomach. More relaxed, she concentrated on the introduction her father was giving her to the head of the Museum Board, a thin, ascetic man named Nate Hinshaw. She met several of the others, a doctor, William Brown, and a large, officious matron her father identified as Ann Manicetti. The woman very obviously admired Maxwell Kirk and ignored Amanda to strike up a one-sided conversation with him.

At that moment, Amanda saw Colin. He stood with a group of men talking together in front of the table, but he was watching her. He lifted his glass in a silent salute, and she inclined her head. His eyes flickered away to his companions, and she was grateful for that. She had been right when she had told Susan he was like a stranger. Seeing him here, she felt nothing at all. He looked at home in these surroundings, of course, for he had always taken pride in dressing well. His wheat-colored hair and handsome features set him apart from the other men present, most of whom were older. But now, with a cool detachment that came from her lack of emotion, she saw the quick mobility of his features, the way his eyes flashed from one speaker to another, his chameleon smile. He was adaptable, and more than a little transparent, she realized with clarity.

After a few minutes, they were seated at the table, and the waiters began to wheel in the steaming bowls of clam chowder on trolleys. Reid Buchanan still had not arrived. His empty chair stood at Amanda's elbow. She alternated between a strange feeling of letdown—she had braced herself for a hurricane that had dissipated before it arrived —and a relief he wasn't there. She took up her spoon to taste the steaming soup, telling herself she would be glad for her father if Reid Buchanan did not arrive at all. Her father sat on her right with the redoubtable Mrs. Manicetti on his other side. Colin, on Mrs. Manicetti's other side, plied the older woman with charm and smiles whenever she turned away from Kirk.

When the meal was over and the waiters had cleared the tables, Nate Hinshaw rose to his feet. "It appears that—" He stopped speaking, and the chair beside Amanda moved back over the heavy carpeting. She didn't need the glimpse of long, muscular legs clad in black trousers to know that Reid Buchanan had arrived and was settling into the chair next to her. Her nerves, alive in every ending, would have told her just as well.

Hinshaw smiled at Buchanan. "I was just about to express to everyone my regret that you weren't able to be with us, Reid. And I was going to give my thanks to you *in absentia* for the delicious meal you made possible for us."

"My pleasure," the husky male voice just behind her left ear said. "I'm glad it was satisfactory."

"More than satisfactory," Hinshaw replied. His eyes moved to Amanda. "I think you know everyone here except perhaps Amanda Kirk, Maxwell's daughter."

There was a silence as everyone waited for her to turn to him. At last she did so, her heart beating heavily.

"My pleasure," he murmured again, his eyes alight with dancing amusement.

"It's nice to see you again, Mr. Buchanan," she said coolly.

Nate Hinshaw smiled and resumed speaking, but the words might have been exotic and foreign for all Amanda understood of them. She was acutely aware of Buchanan's gray eyes on her. She felt as if they were touching the

70

profile of her face, the curve of her neck, which was highly visible with her hair pulled up to her crown in the way that she normally wore it.

She strained to sit still in her chair, giving an impression of calm. She could feel her father's nervous movements beside her. He had lost whatever poise he had had the moment Reid Buchanan had entered the room. When at last Hinshaw finished speaking and allowed her father to take the floor, Amanda knew his nerves were strung to a high pitch.

Maxwell Kirk began to speak in a halting manner that tore at Amanda's soul. His hand movements were quick and nervous as he explained how he would shore up the old building with prestressed concrete to withstand the possible shock from earthquake. He fumbled with his briefcase to produce his drawings, knocking another sheaf of papers out to scatter on the floor. Amanda was out of her chair at once to pick them up, and she heard him resume talking, pointing out how the building would be built to fit the rolling elevation of the land. She slipped back in her chair as he finished giving dimensions and possible alternative uses for some of the rooms and then quoted the price at which he would do the work. He stood, propping the drawings on the edge of the table, looking around at the group. "Are there any questions?"

"That sounds absolutely wonderful, Max," Ann Manicetti enthused, and Amanda liked her for it at once. "Yours is absolutely the best plan of any we've reviewed so far and much more reasonable—"

The woman's sentence was cut off by the cold sound of Reid Buchanan's voice.

"Mr. Kirk," he said. Amanda had never before heard her father's name pronounced as if it were an insult. "It

71

seems to me your estimated cost for this project is far too low. Your anxious desire to do the work is . . . commendable. But what assurance does the committee have that you can actually do the work at the figure you've quoted?"

Her father grasped the cardboard drawings, his knuckles whitening. "If the contract is signed, that's the final price. You know that as well as I do."

"I also know contractors who start a job and then ask the client to renegotiate the fee, knowing the client has no alternative but to agree since the contractor is on the site and has the job started."

"Perhaps *you* do," Maxwell Kirk replied, his words openly hostile, "but my company doesn't operate that way."

Reid Buchanan ignored the jab. "I also know, Mr. Kirk," he drawled, "that you can't possibly complete the job at the price you've quoted us—and still make a profit."

Maxwell Kirk paled. Amanda looked up into his drawn face and felt anger flood her veins, sending heat through every cell of her body. She longed for the kind of masculine strength that could flatten Reid Buchanan with one well-placed blow.

Her father said, "My company isn't a conglomerate like yours. We don't have to charge an exorbitant price to get a job done."

An electric stillness shimmered in the room. Reid Buchanan's voice was soft and incisive. "We don't charge exorbitant prices, Kirk, nor do we construct condominiums that fall into the bay."

Her father stiffened as if he had received a blow to the solar plexus. "My company was misled about the stability of the land—"

"You're the head of that company, Kirk. Every phase

of that construction was your responsibility." He paused and then added, "You know that as well as I do," his soft words echoing her father's with a rapier-sharp thrust of irony.

Amanda sat cold and chilled, knowing this was the thing that had brought her father to the brink of financial ruin. Somehow both Susan and her father had kept her from knowing about the disaster that had happened to her father. No wonder he had no new contracts! No client wanted a company that built buildings that fell down.

Maxwell Kirk loosened his death grip on his drawings and began to put them in his briefcase. He stood straight, his eyes on Nate Hinshaw, who sat across the table with his arms folded on his chest, his face closed. "Nate, you know I was cleared of negligence charges. I . . . Buchanan's accusations are grossly unfair."

Nate Hinshaw raised one dark eyebrow. "I'm afraid I can't agree, Max. I think they are quite justifiable. We can't afford an accident of any kind. The Museum will be partially open to the public even during the renovation. We can't afford so much as a falling board."

Amanda heard the click of the catch on her father's briefcase and felt the brush of his hand on her shoulder. "I think we may as well go, Amanda. It seems a decision has already been reached."

He turned, his head lifted with a dignity that made Amanda love him more than ever. She half rose in her chair, and Ann Manicetti made a sound of dismay.

"Mr. Kirk," Reid Buchanan said, his voice arresting her. "Do you always give up so easily?"

Kirk turned to his antagonist, and Amanda sank back into her chair, holding her breath. In a strained voice, her father said, "I don't indulge in corporate games, Mr. Buchanan, so I'm afraid I don't know the rules."

"Oh, come now," the faintly mocking voice chided. "You've been in the business a long time. Surely you know a lost battle doesn't mean the end of the war." There was a silence and then Buchanan went on. "If we had continued our discussion, I would have asked you for some assurance about your quality control and safety measures, just as I would any other bidder. Both of these things are extra and costly. I would then have suggested that you resubmit a higher bid—a more realistic one—at the earliest possible date. But if you're not interested in doing so . . ."

Amanda's father stared at Buchanan, visibly fighting to maintain control. "I'll do that."

A murmur broke out in the room as approval of the compromise was expressed. Someone—Amanda wasn't sure who—made a suggestion that the committee review Maxwell Kirk's revised bid at the meeting next week. There was another suggestion that the meeting come to a close. And then it was all over. Several of the men rose and Mrs. Manicetti got up too, laughing nervously at something Colin had said. Under cover of the general conversation, her father said, "Amanda, let's go."

Keeping his voice equally low, Reid Buchanan murmured, "Don't go yet, Miss Kirk. I want to talk to you."

"We have nothing to say to each other," she said, ice in her voice.

His swiftness as he gripped her wrist, pinning it to the arm of the chair, caught her off guard. Her father, unaware of her dilemma, had already turned his back and was almost at the door. Pale with anger, she stared at Reid's dark face. "Take your hand off my arm."

74

His fingers bit into her skin. "I once granted you a similar request . . . under similar circumstances."

Her father, discovering her absence, had turned to search the room for her. "Let go of me," she said, keeping her voice under iron control. "My father needs me."

"No," he said calmly. "Tell him you're staying. I want to talk to you about Susan." Just as suddenly as he had captured her wrist, he set it free. "Tell him you're staying."

She stared at him, frustrated once more with a longing to somehow cause this man bodily harm. Amanda, who abhorred violence and had always avoided conflict, was shocked by the hot wave of anger that now surged through her. She rose and paced the few steps that took her to her father's side.

"Go ahead without me, Dad," she told him. "I'm going to talk with Mr. Buchanan for a few minutes."

Any color he had regained in the last few minutes drained away from his face. "What about?"

"Susan," she said shortly. "She's going to visit Mrs. Buchanan for the weekend." To ask her father to join them was now out of the question, as it was for Amanda, too.

"Tomorrow?" Maxwell Kirk said in disbelief.

Amanda nodded. "I'll . . . I'll explain it all to you when I get home, Dad."

He studied her for a long moment and then said, "All right, Amanda. I'll see you this evening." He turned slowly, heavily, and went out the door. She watched him go and felt sick with cold anger, which was not lessened by turning around and seeing that Colin had remained behind.

Reid Buchanan stood idly leaning against the back of

the curved sofa as Colin came to her side and touched her arm. "Amanda, I'm sorry." His back was to Buchanan, but he dropped his voice even lower. "I warned your father this might happen—"

"Yes, I know. Thank you." Wearily, Amanda pushed back a red-gold tendril that had escaped her bun and was clinging to her temple.

"I wanted to explain why I haven't called—" Colin began.

She interrupted, "That isn't necessary."

"But it is," he insisted. "I wanted to see you—"

"I'm sorry," she said. "I've been very busy," giving him a graceful out.

He didn't take it. "Please, Amanda. I've always felt guilty—"

"I don't want you to," she said coolly. "You fell in love with someone else. We're lucky it didn't happen after we were married." Over Colin's shoulder Amanda could see Reid Buchanan in his black silk shirt and black trousers, his arms folded, his eyes hooded, as he stood watching them. *The devil waits.*

"I don't want to talk about it, Colin. You . . . you did what you thought was best for you . . . and Lisa. There's nothing left to say, except that I wish you every happiness."

Her green eyes cool, she stepped away from Colin's restraining hand easily. Some perverse corner of her mind compared his light touch with the steel grip that had kept her in her seat moments ago.

"Then at least let me take you home," Colin pleaded. "I want to see you, talk to you for a few moments—"

"She's staying here, Brent." Short and concise, the words seemed to carry a wealth of meaning.

Colin flushed and turned around to face Buchanan. "What do you mean, she's staying here?"

"What do you think I mean?" The mocking words were heavy with implication.

Colin took a step toward him. "If you harm her in any way more than you already have by crucifying her father —"

Buchanan didn't move a muscle. "What will you do, Brent?"

Colin stood, clenching his fists at his side. "Keep your hands off her."

"Amanda is staying of her own free will."

"Why, you bastard," Colin grated, and took a step toward him, blindly swinging out. In one movement, Reid caught Colin's arm and twisted it, turning Colin's back against his chest, Colin's other arm pinned at his side. The younger man was at once helpless and impotent, and his cries of anguish came more from humiliation than from pain. Buchanan walked him to the door and deposited him—still on his feet—none too gently in the hallway. He leaned against the doorway and studied Colin, who glared at him with malevolent eyes. "Get anything together that you have pertaining to my affairs and send it to my office, Brent. By courier."

"With pleasure," Colin said with sneering emphasis. "Just remember what I said about Amanda. Don't—"

"Amanda is no longer your concern."

"I care about her—"

Reid Buchanan straightened up. Amanda could see the tension in his lithe body by the way the dark silk strained across his shoulders. "You tossed her aside and declared your love for another woman with such speed that she was

77

the target of gossip and speculation for weeks. Is that how you care for her?"

How had he known that? Amanda knew she hadn't told him.

Colin flushed, his tanned skin turning a deep red. "Amanda understood—"

"No doubt she *did,*" came the smooth reply. "She probably considered it a lucky escape." The tone harsher now, he said, "Get out of here, Brent. And stay away from Amanda."

Colin clenched his fists at his sides and stared at Amanda over Reid's shoulder. She felt a mixture of emotions—pity, anger, frustration—but she held herself under tight control. Colin was no match for Buchanan, and her one desire was for Colin to leave before he did, indeed, get hurt. Even though he was younger than Reid by several years, she had just seen how ill-prepared he was to defend himself.

When she made no move toward him, his face darkened. "All right, I'm going. But just remember what I've said, Buchanan."

"And you remember what I've said. She isn't your concern now. You have a wife, Brent."

Colin glared at Buchanan, and then with one last glance at Amanda he turned and walked out of her path of vision. She heard his fast footfalls as he walked purposely away.

Reid Buchanan closed the door. Something alien glittered in his eyes as he looked at Amanda standing in the middle of the room, her face pale, her chin lifted, her slim body clad in the trim gray suit she had worn to travel in that first day. He made an impatient gesture with his hand toward the couch. "Won't you sit down?" She shook her head.

"Would you like a drink?" he asked.

She stared at him. "No."

A ghost of a smile played around his mouth. "If you don't mind, I think I'll have one." He walked to the table and poured himself a measure of Scotch. Then he wandered to the window, his back to her, the table between them. "I suppose you wouldn't believe me if I told you I had your father's best interest in mind as well as the Museum's?"

"No," she said, and then added bitterly, "why should you care what I believe?"

"Damn it, because I do!" He pivoted and set the glass down on the table, facing her, his mouth taut, his eyes glittering. "Do you think I enjoy slashing people apart?"

"I don't think about you at all," she said coolly.

Softly, savagely, he said, "And I've thought of nothing else but you since I left this room a week ago."

Something beat at the sides of her rib cage, clamoring to get out, begging to be released. But she clamped down on it ruthlessly. "Then I suggest you stop," she said coldly. "There's no future in it."

"But there is," he contradicted her softly, his voice intent.

"I . . . no."

"Yes," he said insistently. "We're going to be related soon, you and I, by marriage."

Her throat constricted. "No," she said, her voice low. "Susan and David's marriage makes you Susan's in-law, not mine."

He shrugged as if it were not important. "You're right, of course." He picked up his glass again and tilted it to his mouth. He grimaced as he set the glass on the table. "Scotch on an empty stomach. I used to know better."

Instinctively polite, she said, "You haven't eaten lunch?"

He shook his head. "Or breakfast, or dinner last night if I remember correctly. I vaguely recall some stale sandwiches around two thirty yesterday afternoon."

"At that rate, you'll kill yourself before you're forty," she said, her tone astringent.

His eyes glimmered at her. "That would be a cause for rejoicing in some quarters, wouldn't it?"

She looked at the darkly intelligent face, the lithe body that was still alive with a vibrant energy though he looked travel-weary, and she felt a sharp pang of distaste. "I could never wish . . . anyone dead."

His smile mocked her hesitation. "Not even me? Well, that's a start, at least. Might your largesse extend to having a walking lunch with me at the wharf? Only in the interest of my continued good health, of course. I don't like to eat alone."

"I couldn't eat a thing—"

"I'll eat, you talk," he interjected quickly.

She should refuse, she knew she should. But she looked into those eyes that were probably open only through force of will and said, "I . . . I'll come with you for a few minutes."

The taut mouth relaxed. "I'll get a jacket."

The sun was warm, however, and they left their jackets in the car when they arrived a half hour later at the Embarcadero. They walked along the concrete sidewalk in the carnival atmosphere of crowds and hawkers selling balloons. Reid bought a "walkaway cocktail" of crab and shrimp and a slice of sourdough bread. They strolled away from the open-air restaurant in companionable silence, Reid nibbling the warm shellfish and bread.

The bay glittered in front of them, making the air sea-scented and enticing them toward one of the piers. Boats riding on the surface of the water at a lower level than the dock tugged at their moorings with the wash of the water, their masts thrust up to the level of the handrail. A man, his hair a dusty gray, his face scored with weather lines, sat cross-legged on the dock, mending a net. The wooden shuttle flew back and forth, a long skein of hemp trailing behind it, in and out of the tangle of fish net that lay over his legs. A girl, probably around five or six years of age, Amanda thought, skipped out to watch him. A clown strolled by and proferred his bouquet of balloons, but she lifted dark eyes and sadly shook her head. Reid handed his cup to Amanda and brought a bill from his pocket. He asked the little girl's color preference and soberly bought her the desired red one. Amanda watched as the girl took it from him, thanked him shyly, and ran away to show her gift to her mother.

"That was kind of you," Amanda said coolly. Reid's mouth turned up at the corners. She returned his cup of fish, careful not to touch his hand.

"It's tedious being an ogre every minute," he said, a glitter of amusement in his eyes. "I like to vary my style occasionally."

"You're not an ogre," she said, turning to look out over the bay.

"No? You thought so this afternoon." Something in his voice made her glance at him, and then she wished she hadn't, for he was looking at her with a directness that was disturbing. "Would you like a taste?" he said. She knew the only way was to allow him to put the tidbit between her lips with his fingers.

"No, thank you," she said, and turned to walk away

81

from him, ignoring his mocking smile, letting her feet carry her farther out on the pier. Her footsteps made hollow sounds against the boards. *The sounds of retreat,* she thought wryly. The soft *chunk, chunk* of the boats as they tugged at their moorings along the sides seemed to echo and agree.

But her escape was only temporary. Reid came to stand beside her and stare out over the water, his eyes narrowed. He had finished eating and the cup was gone. Somehow, so was the softened, approachable man. This was the hard executive, the shrewd planner, who stood beside her under the soft blue sky, watching a sea gull float lazily above and catch a freewheeling ride on an air current that lifted it toward Alcatraz.

"I've called my mother," he said unexpectedly. "She's looking for us. We'll leave around seven o'clock tomorrow morning."

"I'll tell Susan," she said.

"You'll both be ready?"

"I . . . I won't be going." She turned to look at him. His face was a mask.

"So you came with me today to tell me that."

She didn't deny it.

A muscle moved in his jaw, and he said as if she had answered him, "Because of what I said to your father?"

"That among other things."

His voice was soft, derisive. "What other things?"

She shook her head, not daring to voice it, staring away from him over the water once again. His hand, long-fingered and gentle, reached for a drift of hair that had escaped her bun and floated near her earlobe. Little flames of alarm shot along her skin where his fingers touched her, and instinctively she stepped back almost to the edge of the pier, wedged between him and the guardrail.

"You little fool," he grated, reaching for her with both hands. "Would you rather take a dunking than have me touch you?"

His hands on her bare arms sent a starburst of feeling through her. It was as if she had always known how his hands would feel: warm, strong, and completely right. Light and life rose in her . . . and desire. She was swept up in its crest; it was as if a million years ago they had known each other and stood like this in the drowsy warmth of the sun with the taste of the sea salt on her lips and the sharp cry of a gull overhead.

"Look at me, Amanda."

The husky command with its intimate caress warned her not to, but she couldn't help herself. When she raised her eyes, he saw the surrender and the need at once. His own dark pupils flared as though a super nova were eclipsing the silver irises. She was powerless to stop the descent of that male mouth. He took her lips slowly with a sureness that opened her soul like a crack in a dam. She felt only a trickle at first, but then his lips sent sensual life flooding into every nerve cell of her body. It was like a roaring river that had been restrained too long and had gained awesome power from the restraint. Too long had she denied the passion in her nature, too long had she cloaked her feminine needs in a shell of reserve. Now she was tossed on the rapids of his kiss, completely in the spell of the man whose mouth was pressed against her own, tasting her lips, exploring their fullness and delicate curves and then parting them to savor the deeper sweetness within. When she thought she would be totally destroyed, he lifted his head.

"Yes"—he breathed softly—"I knew you would taste like that."

His words were a jarring reminder that he had tasted many women's lips. She strained against him, pushing at his chest with her hands, but the movement only locked her hips against his muscular thighs. He slid his palms to the small of her back. There was a sound like a grunt, and Reid smiled. "The old man approves."

She had forgotten the old man, forgotten everything except the man who held her. Now the cold touch of reality crept through her. "Reid, let go of me."

He only brought her close enough to brush her temple with his lips. "No," he murmured. "Not yet."

His lips brushed the soft skin just below her ear, and she knew she was in danger of sinking under the spell of his sensual power all over again. "I won't be one of your coterie of women," she said huskily.

"One kiss hardly qualifies you," he murmured against her forehead, his words spoken with dry humor.

She thought of the qualifications—lying naked next to him—and pushed against his chest with such force that he was caught by surprise. She stepped out of his arms and stood flushed, watching the lazy smile form on his mouth, the mouth that had almost destroyed her.

"Colin was right," she said clearly and coolly. "You are a bastard."

The lazy smile hardened into ironic brilliance. "He would know."

"Compared to you, he's a saint," Amanda flared.

His mouth twisted. "Is that what you think?"

Before she could answer, the old man grunted again, this time with disgust. Unwilling to be the source of his entertainment any longer, Amanda turned and walked away from Reid, her heels clicking on the wooden boards.

He was beside her before she had taken three steps. "Where are you going?"

"Back to Dad's office."

He took hold of her elbow and stopped her in midstep, turning her to face him. "I won't always let you run away from me, Amanda."

She lifted her head. "No," she said, "because this won't happen again."

"You don't really believe that," he said, taking her elbow and walking with her in the direction of his car.

She paced in stiff silence beside him, refusing to be drawn into a senseless round of contradiction. When they reached the car, he helped her into its dark luxury and walked around with his lithe stride to slide in behind the wheel. He inserted the key in the ignition, but instead of starting the car, he lifted one lean hand to her chin.

She sat fighting her body's instinctive response to his warm fingers, staring back at him coolly and unmoving.

"Your forces are badly divided, Amanda," he said, "for you to be declaring war."

"I don't know what you're talking about," she said, lying.

"You know exactly what I'm talking about, Amanda Kirk," he said calmly. "You know you're not indifferent to me, no matter how much you deny it."

His finger stroked the smooth line of her throat, and a warm tingling was left in the wake of his touch. With intense effort, she sat unmoving. "You have superb discipline," he murmured. "I admire that." His questing finger sought and found the erratic pulse at the base of her throat. "But you can't control your heart, Amanda."

Before she could move away, he bent his head and pressed his lips to the erotic spot his fingers had caressed to an ultra-sensitized state. "You see," he said softly, murmuring against the silken skin at the hollow of her throat, "I have my own truth drug."

It was only another reminder of his expertise. With the certain knowledge that any involvement with Reid Buchanan would be twice as painful, twice as devastating as her engagement to Colin, she struggled desperately to think. No longer able to defend herself by her own will, she retreated to the one thing her reeling mind told her Reid would never tolerate. "You're very sure of yourself . . . aren't you?" she asked huskily. "How do you know I'm not—" She took a sharp, indrawn breath as his lips wandered lower, tracing the line of her opened collar and still lower, into the hollow of her breasts. Closing her eyes against an ache of longing, she ran her tongue over dry lips and forced herself to continue. "How do you know I'm not thinking of Colin when you kiss me?"

The enormity of her lie amazed her, and she was even more amazed that Reid did not guess at once she was lying. He drew back and stared at her, his eyes narrowed, cold anger turning them steel-gray. "I'll have to devise a way for you to be able to distinguish between us." He inspected her heightened color, the creamy perfection of her skin, the proud lift of her head, as though he were studying a particularly offensive laboratory specimen. Then he swooped, gathering her to him with no tenderness at all, his hands hard and grasping on her shoulders and back, his muscular body pressed against hers. He took her mouth with a cold passion that insulted as it possessed, degraded as it burned.

With ruthless intensity his lips parted her own, his

tongue plunging deep to taunt and tantalize her in a way that left Amanda breathless. Struggling to remain unresponsive, her hand moved up to press flat against his chest, her fingertips just grazing the bare, warm skin and silky hair exposed above his open collar. A wave of desire suddenly and swiftly washed her defenses away. Her fingers wandered higher, moving along the smoothly muscled column of his neck. The gesture that began as one of resistance had somehow changed into something more like a caress. She felt herself relax beneath his weight and softly moaned against the pressure of his lips, no longer able to suppress her response, to hide the deep and intense sensual arousal Reid's kiss had awakened in her.

At last, he released her. He inspected the damage his kiss had done with satisfaction, smiling sardonically at her bruised and swollen lips, the fiery glitter in her eyes.

"Yes," he said, nodding. "I thought that should do it."

"You arrogant, conceited—" she began.

He laughed without amusement. "At least you won't confuse me with Colin." He started the car with the self-satisfied smile of a tiger that has just eaten its prey. She sat next to the door, as far away from him as she could, telling herself she hated him with every fiber of her being and trying not to listen to the small corner of her mind that whispered it wasn't so.

CHAPTER 5

It was in a corner of her mind, but it threatened to take over every inch of her consciousness. She helped Susan prepare dinner that evening and sat across from her, listening as the girl told her father about her plans for the weekend. But it was always there, waiting. It needed only to have Susan leave the table to get ready for an evening out with David, and her father, silent and withdrawn, to go into the living room, to spring full-blown within her, re-creating the image of Reid Buchanan, reliving the feel of his mouth on hers and his hands on her skin. . . .

She walked back and forth, carrying the smooth porcelain dishes to the kitchen. She tried to push it down, to thrust the thought of him away from her. What was happening to her? Why had she invited his kiss? And why couldn't she forget it?

The rest of her mind prevaricated. *It's only natural; Reid Buchanan is an attractive and virile man. And you're a woman.* But the other part of her mind laughed. *You've gone out with men like him,* it said, *men as attractive as he is. Not one of them disturbed you in the slightest. Not one of them made your pulse pound as crazily. . . .*

Susan's voice called to her from the living room, lifting her out of her reverie. Amanda walked through the swinging door to see the back of a dark head she was sure was Reid's. She stumbled on the rug, pitching forward against him. He turned around in time to catch her in his arms. Amanda felt like an utter fool. She looked up into eyes that sparkled with amusement, blue eyes, David's eyes. He was very like Reid from the back, but there was not much resemblance in the face. He was years younger, and his curving lips held none of Reid's cynical mockery.

"I've seen pictures of you," David said, slowly releasing her as she regained her balance. "But they didn't do justice to your coloring. Reid was right. You're fantastic."

She flushed, whether from David's compliment or from the knowledge that he had been discussing her with Reid, she didn't know. "Thank you," she said, her voice much cooler than her cheeks, her hands smoothing down her skirt.

"Sure you won't change your mind about coming with us tomorrow?" David asked, smiling. "I know Susan wishes you would go."

Amanda shook her head, sorry he had extended the invitation in front of her father. "I think I'd better stay here."

David shrugged and helped Susan into her wrap. "Well, maybe some other time—after the wedding."

Susan's eyes shone. "Yes, Amanda. David says the ranch is great."

"I'm a working girl," Amanda said lightly. "Perhaps next year."

Susan picked up her small evening bag, kissed her father, and told them good-night and not to wait up.

Amanda returned to the kitchen, conscious of her father's suddenly fixed gaze.

When she finished the dishes and returned, he seemed

to have been waiting for her. Though he sat in a chair next to a lamp table with his briefcase open on his lap, he hadn't touched the contents.

"Dad," she said gently, "why don't you put that away? You've done enough for one day."

"Have I?" he asked, his words carrying an ironic tinge.

She picked up the briefcase and set it on the floor. He made no move to stop her.

"Why did you refuse to go with Susan to see Mrs. Buchanan?"

"Because I didn't want to leave you alone," she said lightly, dropping down on the floor beside his chair.

"When does she leave?"

"Tomorrow morning, at seven."

His eyes moved over her face, her hair. "I want you to go with her, Amanda."

"She doesn't need my protection anymore, Dad."

"No," he said, his voice strangely husky. "But I do." His eyes closed momentarily as if he were in pain. "When I was sure Nate Hinshaw was back in his office this afternoon, I called him. He was pleasant, but noncommittal. I doubt very much if the committee will approve *any* proposal of mine. He didn't say anything definite, of course. He just said he didn't know."

Her father stared at some distant point beyond her shoulder as Amanda sat silent, saying nothing to disturb his thoughts. "I've played at this business for twenty years, Amanda, knowing I didn't really have to make money, knowing that no matter what I did, your mother's legacy would support us. Then she died. I missed her so much that I wanted to give up, just quit. But I couldn't. I had you and Susan. You were a part of her. I wanted to protect you, provide for you both because you . . . you

90

carry the very essence of her into the future. Through you, Amanda, and through Susan, too, Leslie still lives." His eyes seemed to burn into hers. "But I've failed. I've failed miserably. I've got to ask for your help, Amanda, I've got to lean on you as I used to on your mother—"

She watched him with an aching heart, knowing that only the shock and disappointment of the day had lowered the barrier of his natural reticence. He was a man driven to the brink of his endurance.

"You look so much like her, Amanda. More so every day." For years, he had steadfastly refused to discuss his wife. Now it was pouring out as if he had no control over his words at all. "Tonight when young Buchanan complimented you and you blushed, it might have been Leslie standing there." He rubbed one hand across his forehead. "Then you told him you weren't going with them this weekend because you wanted to stay here, and I knew at once why. You were trying to protect me from feeling as if my girls had both deserted me and gone over to the enemy." He sighed, a long, shuddering breath. "The women around me have always protected me. First your mother, then you. Even Susan in her way." He hesitated and added, "Benita, too, protected me, let me live in my own little world." He laughed, a harsh, bitter sound. "There was a building boom right after your mother died, and anyone in the construction business had to be a complete idiot not to prosper. I wasn't a complete idiot, just a partial one—"

"Dad," she said, gripping his hand fiercely. "You're being ridiculous! Your company has always had a reputation for quality building. You've done beautiful homes—"

"And that reputation collapsed in one day, right along with the frames for those apartments. *In one day, Aman-*

da!" A shudder ripped through him. "But, in a way, I was responsible. I was never interested in mass producing apartment complexes. We weren't equipped for it. Thank God, no one was hurt!"

"The committee will recognize and remember that reputation you had for quality, Dad."

Her father shook his head. "They have short memories, just like the rest of the world. They're only interested in results, not some high-minded idea of quality I might have had in the past."

"I refuse to believe they won't give you a second chance," she said loyally.

"Not if Buchanan has his way."

The thought was repugnant. "No—"

Her father looked at her, his eyes suddenly cool and calculating.

Disturbed, she rose and walked to the window to escape his intent stare. But his voice, low and intense, reached out to her from across the room. "Why don't you want to go?"

The lights of San Francisco lay before her, gleaming and mocking.

Her father rose and walked over to her. "He's interested in you, isn't he, Amanda?"

She didn't have to ask whom he meant or pretend she didn't know what he was talking about. She stood silently, wanting desperately to deny it, aching to stop his words.

"He listens to you, Amanda. He listened to you about Susan—"

She shook her head. "No, Dad, he didn't," she said to the lights. "We disagreed. I wanted Susan to wait—"

His hands on her shoulders, he turned her around. "But the ultimate result was the same: Susan's acceptance into the family and an invitation to meet David's mother, something Buchanan had forbidden before. Suppose . . . suppose you could accomplish the same thing for me." Her eyes flew to his face, but he swallowed and went on. "Amanda, I'm only asking you to talk to him. He might listen to what you have to say. Amanda, if there was even the slightest chance that you could soften his position toward me—"

"I couldn't. Dad, don't ask me to do that. . . ."

His eyes glowed down at her. "A moment ago you said the committee would remember my reputation as a quality builder. But they won't. Not unless someone reminds them. And if it were Buchanan, they'd listen."

"Dad, I couldn't . . . couldn't use an invitation to his mother's house to—"

"Amanda, more business is done over cocktails and lunch and dinner than in the office. Buchanan knows that. Do you think he would hesitate if the situation were reversed? You can't expect me to do less when I have so much more at stake. My employees—some of them have worked for me for years. They're older men, Amanda. They'll find it almost impossible to find another job in today's tight market." He paused and took a deep breath. "Buchanan called it war, Amanda, and that's what it is. And if I have to recruit you to fight with me, I'll do it. At least, I'll try. Please, say you'll go and just try to talk to him. That's all I ask, nothing more."

"Dad, I can't."

He took his hands from her shoulders, his face bleak. "All right, Amanda. I understand."

But the sound of his voice and the hunted look in his eyes stayed with her like a picture playing over and over in her head as she showered and got ready for bed. She lay there still and quiet and tormented. The foghorns began their mournful fugue over the water. She had opened a window, and now the curtain blew against the wall, making soft, moving shadows. She felt caught and torn and tortured. She shouldn't have been afraid to help her father, she should have granted his request without a moment's hesitation. But she hadn't. She had refused. She had refused because . . . because she was afraid, desperately afraid. Her world had been cool and calm and free of emotion, just the way she had wanted it for the last year. And it had to remain that way, or she could not survive.

She had known Reid Buchanan less than a week, had seen him only twice. Yet in one short afternoon he had succeeded in penetrating her defenses, taking over her thoughts in a way no other man had done since Colin. *Since Colin!* She couldn't take the chance of being thrown in Reid's company for a weekend, she just couldn't. She knew instinctively that repeated and prolonged exposure to him would destroy her in a way that would make the pain she had suffered over Colin seem minute. She had to stay away from Reid Buchanan to preserve her sanity. But because she was a coward—yes, a stupid, idiotic coward— her father's company might falter and fail.

Amanda shivered, though the room was warm. She pulled the coverlet up to her chin and stared into the darkness, hating herself. She lay awake long after Susan came home and tiptoed around the room in the dark, getting ready for bed. She was still awake when the first light began to slant through the window. There, in the pale light of those first rays, she came to a decision at last and dropped off to sleep.

A few hours later, Susan's alarm began to ring. Amanda tossed the covers back and reached under her bed for her overnight suitcase. She got up and began to pack with an air of cold purpose.

Fog enclosed the airport in a moist blankness that matched Amanda's state of mind exactly. She felt gray as she slid out of the taxi that had brought them to the landing strip. The mist was a cloak wrapping itself around her, keeping her safe, letting her listen to Susan's excited chatter with a numbed sense of inevitability. And the whole idea of safety in the fog didn't make any sense at all. It had to be dangerous to fly in fog like this.

The driver bent over the trunk of the car and handed their luggage to them, the overhead lights giving his face and dark slicker an eerie pink sheen. Amanda paid the fare and watched as he slid quickly behind the wheel of the car, flipped the meter down, and started the engine. Twin beams of light stabbed through the mist as the car turned. Her last line of retreat was gone.

David materialized from somewhere to the side, startling them both. He was surprised and delighted by Amanda's presence, and he kissed them and took their suitcases, tucking Susan's make-up bag under his arm with a mock groan. He guided them toward the airplane, a single-engine Cessna, which was a vague winged shape poised on the runway.

"We're fueled and ready," David said. "Reid will be glad you're prompt."

David swung up the metal steps to carry their luggage on, and Susan followed him. Amanda had almost reached the sanctuary of the plane when a dark shape appeared at the bottom of the steps. It caught at her arm, halting her.

"You changed your mind," that low, mocking voice said.

She had been waiting for this. A quick sweep of her eyes over Reid took in the beads of moisture clinging to the shoulders of his brown leather jacket, the well-worn denims that outlined his muscular legs. The polished executive had vanished, but here was a man infinitely more dangerous.

"I should have called," she said coolly, her pulse pounding. "But I didn't know where I could reach you."

His mouth lifted with amusement. "We could remedy that."

"If my coming is an imposition, I—" She had rushed into speech to close off his innuendo, but as she retreated a step from the plane, his palm flattened against the small of her back and her throat closed.

"It's no imposition," he said smoothly, propelling her up the steps, his hand stealing between her khaki jacket and the waistband of her pants. "It's a surprise. But a very pleasant one."

Amanda settled into a high-backed leather chair, cushiony and comfortable. Susan sat in a similar chair next to her and behind David, who was in the copilot position. David introduced Susan to Reid, and Amanda saw the wary look come into her sister's eyes as she said hello. Reid turned away to make preparations for the take-off, adjusting the headset to his ears. "Is it safe to take off in this fog?" Susan asked nervously, her fingers fumbling with the clip of her seat belt.

David half turned in his seat to reassure her, his glance at his brother also wary and a bit rueful. "Reid can handle it. He filed an instrument flight report, and he'll use the ground-path localizer to keep us in the middle of the runway. Once we're above the fog"—he shrugged and grinned—"there's nothing to it."

"I didn't know your brother was a pilot," Susan said, a trace of a worried frown still on her forehead.

"He's got a pilot's license and an A and P, airframe and power plant license, too. He can fly them and fix them. I haven't got enough hours to qualify."

Reid began talking, requesting permission for take-off. David was quiet as the roar of the engine cut off his further efforts. They began to move, Reid guiding the plane down the middle of the runway, his eyes on the gyro and magnetic compass. Then they were in the air, rising above the fog.

They left the shrouded city behind them. The sun glistened on the foothills, the giant Sequoias, and trapped mountain lakes of icy blue. They flew past the barren peak of Mount Whitney and its sister peaks with the ease and swiftness of an eagle.

Reid no longer talked formally with the tower in San Francisco. His voice had lowered and taken on a lazy, informal tone. Then he was laughing at something the unknown voice in the earphones had said, and the sound sent a shiver over Amanda's skin, it was so full of genuine pleasure.

"Make a pass over Brown's meadow before we land, Reid," David said. "Let's see if anybody's there yet."

The plane dipped slightly to follow a narrow strip of valley barren of trees, its floor a carpet of green, a silver stream winding along its eastern edge.

"There is somebody there," David said excitedly.

A wisp of smoke curled from the brick chimney of a log cabin nestled in a cluster of pine trees. The only building within sight for miles, it faced the meadow. A rail section of fence stood in front of it, and two horses were tethered

97

there, their heads turned slightly as if they were listening to the sound of the plane.

"Where are the cattle?" Susan asked, frowning. "In the barn?"

David laughed. "No, sweet, they're on their way home from the winter range. We graze them in the desert in the wintertime and in the mountains in the summertime." He turned back to Reid. "Want to see if the herd is coming in yet from the Coscos, or will we get picked up as a blip on the naval station's radar?"

"I think they know we're in the area," came the dry reply.

Abruptly, the mountains fell away, and now they saw the desert—sand, scrub brush, and boulders. Cattle, red and sleek with white faces and switching tails, were moving slowly west, being driven by a dozen or so cowboys wheeling and turning about the herd on their horses. One of the men looked up and took his hat off to wave it at them.

"Why do you have two ranges?" Susan asked. "Wouldn't it be easier just to keep the cattle in one place?"

"Sure it would," David answered. "And in a year, they'd have eaten everything in the desert down to the roots. Or if we left them in the mountains, they'd freeze or starve to death in the ten feet of snow that falls up there in the winter. Most cattle ranchers have winter and summer ranges, but Owens Valley is unique, I guess. Mount Whitney is the highest peak in the Sierras and it's thirty miles northwest of us. Get in your car and drive about the same distance southeast and you're in Death Valley."

"And this is where your mother likes to live," Susan said, shuddering slightly.

"She says it's the best of all possible worlds, sunrises

over the mountains and desert sunsets," David replied. "But there are drawbacks. We rent most of our grazing land from the government and that puts a limit on the size of our herd. We figure one cow to three hundred acres of desert scrub. The mountain meadow's another story, of course. We can graze one cow for every two acres up there. But, even so, there's only so much available land, and we share with two other ranchers. One of them is Mom's brother. We generally run about five hundred head a season, which makes this a small operation compared to the big ranches in Texas." He shrugged. "Mom's not interested in expanding. To her, ranching is the best way of life."

Susan looked down at the red backs of the cows that moved in a cloud of dust. "It looks so dry," she said. "Don't cattle get thirsty in the desert?"

David grinned. "We want them to get thirsty. They don't gain weight if they don't drink water. We haul fifty-pound salt blocks out to them just to make sure they do drink plenty of water. We get all we need from natural springs. We pipe the spring water to troughs for the cattle."

"You have your own troughs out there in the desert?" Susan asked, incredulous.

"Our family has been in this valley for over fifty years," David said. "Some of our concrete water troughs were poured into molds by Mom's dad when he first started ranching here. Our worst water problem is desert willow. Its hair roots grow into our pipes, clogging them. We have to get a long rod and clean the pipes periodically. But the cattle know where the troughs are. After the first year, they're range-smart."

The plane circled and a tarmac landing strip appeared

ahead of them. Reid brought the plane down smoothly, jolting them only slightly as he neared the end of the strip and the plane came to a quick halt.

A battered station wagon, its blue paint faded and covered with a thin coat of dust, waited for them. A man leaned against the fender. He wore a hat, and his spare, hard body was dressed in faded denims and a plaid shirt. Amanda stepped out of the plane first, and Susan followed her down the steps. The surface of the runway was smooth under her feet, but beyond it the earth was brick-red, dry and dusty. The cowboy gave a low whistle of appreciation for the girls as he straightened up and headed toward them.

Amanda felt a proprietary hand at her waist and knew from the tingle of her skin that it was Reid behind her. The cowboy, who appeared to be in his early twenties, halted in front of them. His eyes flickered lazily from one girl to another, settling on Amanda. "Quite a pair to draw to, Reid."

"This is Bob Conroy." It was David, carrying the luggage and coming up behind them, who made the introduction. "My fiancée, Susan Kirk, and her sister, Amanda."

Bob Conroy's eyes traveled over Amanda's hair and down the length of her slim body in the khaki pants suit. "He did say it's your sister who is David's girl, didn't he?"

"Why aren't you watching the house?" Reid asked, his tone grim.

Bob Conroy shrugged casually, but there was a glint in the blue eyes. "Your mother deputized me to meet you," he said. "She didn't want the women getting their feet dusty." His smile broadened as he looked at the pale color of Amanda's trouser suit. "Though I can't say they'll be much better off in old Betsy." He nodded toward the car.

"Sorry we couldn't offer you anything better. Cathrene took the Datsun into Olancha to pick up some things for Jane."

Reid's mouth tightened. "It doesn't matter," Amanda said, stepping forward to ease the tension since it was her clothes that were under discussion. "We're not afraid of dust."

"Yes, let's go, Conroy," David said impatiently from behind Susan, holding a suitcase. "These things aren't getting any lighter."

They walked toward the car, clouds of brick-red dust lifting under their feet. David put the luggage in the back and handed Susan in the rear door, bending his long frame to climb in behind her. That left Amanda to slide in the front seat next to Conroy. Reid followed her, his mouth twisting. Bob started the motor, and after a few protesting coughs he managed to turn the car around and head down a rough track toward a grove of trees and a cluster of buildings that seemed to be the only high point for miles around. The rest was brown earth and green meadows. Amanda looked out the window, trying to enjoy the sight of endless, open land and mountains behind, but she was supremely conscious of the young cowboy's thigh next to hers. She shifted slightly, and Reid lifted his arm to lay it on the top of the seat near her shoulders to give her more room, but that only had the effect of drawing her closer to *him*.

"Don't leave the house again, under any circumstances," Reid ordered peremptorily, and then, "When will the herd get to the ranch?"

With what Amanda thought was cheerful animosity, Conroy said, "We should have them in the home corrals by tonight," and wheeled the car onto the curving driveway with lazy ease.

Reid said, "Good," but he didn't sound pleased. The car stopped and he got out. Amanda slid across the seat and stepped to the sidewalk to face the house that Reid Buchanan, tycoon and tyrant, had lived in as a boy. It was truly a ranch house—one story, low and rambling, its clapboards painted a soft gray color. Cottonwood and poplar trees clustered around it. The house had a solidness, a permanence, as if the people who lived here in the shadow of the mountains and the reach of the desert were made of stronger will and flesh than ordinary mortals.

Inside the house, Amanda's sense of permanence intensified. A family might have lived and loved in this room for a hundred years. The knotty pine walls were timeless, and the golden oak floor glowed with wax and many polishings. Plaid chairs and sofas with wide wooden arms, chosen for ease and comfort rather than decoration, stood about the room, and a fireplace that made nonsense of the modern kind soared up the height of the wall opposite Amanda. A man could have stood in its curved brick opening and the sand-colored rock face took up nearly the length of the wall. A white fur rug lay on the floor in front of it.

But Amanda forgot the room at once when a woman stepped into it from a back doorway. If she had had a picture of Reid's mother in her mind, it was that of a tall, austere female, someone cool and unbending. This woman was nothing like that. Short, almost tiny, slim-hipped and full-bosomed in a pants suit of a soft biscuit color, she seemed to be openly amused and pleased.

There was nothing at all to remind Amanda of Reid, but

as the woman stepped closer she saw that the amusement did not hide the gray eyes that took in every inch of her.

She grasped Amanda and pressed cool lips to her cheek, startling her. "I'm glad to meet you, Susan—"

The lazy drawl behind her said, "This isn't Susan. This is Amanda, her older sister."

Amanda caught a whiff of lavender as Mrs. Buchanan lifted her head toward Reid with an indescribable expression in her eyes.

"*This* is Susan," David said, catching her by the arm and leading her forward. Mrs. Buchanan's gaze was just as assessing as she studied the girl, and there was no embarrassment in her manner as she leaned forward and bestowed a kiss on Susan's cheek.

"I thought my boys couldn't play tricks on me anymore," she said, smiling, "but you see they still can. Did you have a good flight?"

"It was marvelous," Susan replied, with shining eyes. "I've never flown before."

"You haven't?" Jane Buchanan said, her eyes flickering back to Reid. "Were you careful, son?"

Reid's answer was lazily amused. "You know I'm always careful."

"Oh? I can remember the time when you weren't," came the tart reply.

David laughed. "There was a cattle buyer from Texas who had just lost his wife," he explained. "We thought he was more interested in seeing Mother than the cattle. Reid brought him out from the city last fall. But it seems big brother kept hitting air pockets all the way over the mountains. The fellow was green when he got here and couldn't wait to hire a car and drive to Vegas to fly home."

"All that maneuvering was wasted, son," Jane Buchanan said and chuckled. "He wasn't my type."

Reid glanced around the room as if he had something else on his mind. "Where's Tessa?"

"Sick in bed with the summer flu."

"John?" Reid asked.

His mother nodded. "He's got it, too. Didn't Bob tell you?" She turned to the girls. "John is my foreman and Tessa is his wife and my housekeeper."

Reid scowled darkly. "You mean John's not heading the roundup?"

"That's exactly what I mean," Jane Buchanan said calmly.

"Well, who is?" came the impatient demand.

"Tim."

There was a short, tense silence in the room. "You're letting a fifteen-year-old boy have the responsibility of finding and separating five hundred head of cattle from a thousand others?"

"He's not out there by himself, you know."

Reid turned to David. "Show the girls to their rooms. I'm going over to see John."

Jane Buchanan stepped in his path, a diminutive woman he could have tossed aside with one hand. "No, you're not." Her eyes sparkled with determination and there was iron in her voice. "John has just gone to bed, finally, after a week of stumbling around ill and pretending he *wasn't.* I won't have you going over there and preying on his already overworked sense of responsibility toward me. You stay away from him, Reid Buchanan!"

Silkily, lazily, he said, "Is that a direct order from the boss?"

Mother stood looking up at son. "That's exactly what

it is." Her voice was crisp. "I won't have you interfering. We get along most of the time without you very well, so don't think you're going to come here now and order us around just because we've had a little trouble. Save that for those executives you keep busy in the city." Her eyes went to Amanda, and then she said to Reid, "If you want to make yourself useful, get whatever you need out of your room and take it in to David's. Susan will have the spare room across from me as I'd planned, but the other spare room is occupied and I'll have to put Amanda in your room."

"I shouldn't have come," Amanda murmured. "I didn't realize—"

"Nonsense," Jane Buchanan retorted. "There's no trouble."

"Who's in the other spare room?" Reid asked.

"Janie," Mrs. Buchanan answered.

Reid made an exasperated sound. "You're supposed to take it easy," he said, scowling, "not run a ranch single-handedly and baby-sit a seven-year-old."

"I couldn't let her stay in the same house with John and Tessa," his mother replied. "They're both too ill to look after her. Now mind your manners and take your guests to their rooms. They might want to freshen up a bit before we have our midmorning coffee."

There was an angry set to his shoulders as he turned and plucked Amanda's suitcase from David's hand. "This way," he growled, turning toward the hall. Amanda would have given anything to have sunk into a hole in the floor.

Susan's room was done in soft mint green, the furniture dark with a patina of age and loving care. Amanda hoped that the unfortunate Tessa had prepared for Susan's visit rather than Mrs. Buchanan. David followed the younger girl into the room, carrying her suitcase. After glancing around, Amanda reluctantly followed Reid down the hall to a room diagonally opposite.

Reid Buchanan had not grown up with luxury. It was a spartan, male domain that he led her into, and Amanda knew instinctively that nothing here had been changed from his school days. The dresser held a brush set that must have been his at a very early age. Her eyes went to the single bed with its Indian-design coverlet done in soft shades of salmon and turquoise. Reid lifted her suitcase to a stand at the foot of his bed and turned to her, his eyes still carrying the remnants of his anger.

"I'm sorry," she said, her cheeks warm with color. "I shouldn't have come."

"Perhaps you shouldn't have," he agreed enigmatically, "but not because you're turning me out of my bed."

"Then take us back—"

"No." The word was clipped.

"Really," Amanda began, "we're imposing. And your mother's health—"

She was almost pleading in her desperation to be away from this room that held the strength of him, the core of his personality. It was so overwhelming, it seemed to permeate through her skin to her bones.

His metallic eyes sliced at her. "No." As if to release his anger, he turned his back and walked to the bureau to open a drawer with excessive force. He began to remove jeans and shirts, the leather jacket sliding over his shoulders as he finished and slammed the drawer shut. When he turned to face her, his face was taut. "The purpose of this visit was to gain better understanding between the Kirk family and the Buchanan family. How do you think it will improve my mother's health to learn that the woman my brother has chosen to marry—and her sister— want to leave at once because the housekeeper isn't on hand to cater to their every whim?"

Color flooded Amanda's cheeks. "You know that isn't true!"

"My mother doesn't." He studied her with no apparent contrition. "Having run a household for a number of years, you must know something about it. You could help."

"Yes, of course," she said stiffly.

"It's our custom to have a big meal at the end of the drive. Do you think you could take charge of it?"

The lazy words were a gauntlet thrown at her.

"Yes," she said coolly.

His lips lifted in something of a smile. "Good. Plan it for around eight o'clock. We may be later, but we won't be earlier."

"You're going out there with them?"

"What's the matter, Amanda?" He leaned back against the bureau smiling, his hands holding his clothing. "Are you afraid I've forgotten how to handle a horse?"

She didn't think that at all. She doubted there was anything he couldn't handle with those lean, competent hands. He had certainly handled her! But she had thought of him for so long as the angry, powerful executive she had first met, it was difficult to picture him on a horse chasing a cow through the desert scrub.

There was a cooling of the anger in his eyes. "My mother doesn't want me to boss her around, but she won't object to a couple of extra range hands. You'll have to keep Susan occupied. David will be with me for the next twelve hours or so." He gathered up his clothing and walked to a closet to reach inside and pull out a pair of well-worn oxblood boots.

Stung by his tone and the implication that they were children who had to be entertained constantly, she said, "We're grown women. We can manage without your august presence."

He straightened and gazed at her. Her breath seemed to stick in her throat. "I didn't need to be reminded that you're a woman, Amanda," he said mockingly, "but you have the tendency of a child to run at the first sign of trouble."

"I don't know what you're talking about," she said sharply, but he took two steps toward her so that he was almost touching her. His hands were full of clothes and boots, but she felt threatened by his nearness. "Don't you? Did you think I didn't know your sudden desire to run back to the city was prompted by the fear I might steal in here in the middle of the night and reclaim my bed with you in it?"

"Don't be ridiculous," she said coolly, her heart hammering against her throat as she fought down a vivid image of his words. "I never once thought—"

"Didn't you?" His face dark with sardonic pleasure, he said, "Then I suggest you think about it." He lifted an eyebrow and laughed. "We both know that's why you came, Amanda."

"Why, you—" She stared defiantly up at him, the color flooding her cheeks. He laughed and then stepped into the hallway. She glared after him, clenching her fists and fighting the urge to walk to his bureau, pick up his own silver brush, and fling it straight at that dark head.

CHAPTER 6

Later that morning, Amanda stood in the kitchen discussing the preparations for the evening meal with Jane Buchanan. She had almost succeeded in putting Reid Buchanan's disturbing presence out of her mind—until she met Cathrene Taylor. The dark-haired girl appeared in the back doorway of the kitchen.

"I knocked, but no one answered," she said in a throaty tone and walked into the room with a familiarity that suggested she was a frequent visitor. She carried two large brown bags in her arms, and she stepped forward to set them on the yellow counter. "There's your groceries, Jane." The girl wore immaculate jeans that hugged her hips and a red shirt of silk that clung to her full breasts as she straightened. "Is this David's fiancée?"

Jane Buchanan shook her head and introduced Amanda, but Cathrene made no attempt to extend her hand or hide her boredom once she learned Amanda was not engaged to David. At the first pause, she asked impatiently, "Where's Reid?" Long, dark-red nails lifted to push a strand of hair back. "I wanted to say hello."

"He's out helping with the roundup," Jane said, her words laconic, her tone saying volumes.

"Well, I suppose I could stop by again later. . . ." She

frowned, and then for the first time blue eyes framed by exquisite dark lashes swung to Amanda. Cathrene Taylor was displeased, and somehow Amanda was to blame.

"Yes, do that, Cathrene," Jane Buchanan said, a shrewd and thoughtful look on her face. "I'm sure David will want you to meet Susan."

There was silence as Cathrene continued to scrutinize Amanda, examining every thread of her plaid blouse, her denim trousers. Then, unexpectedly, she shrugged. "I'll look forward to it." She swung out of the kitchen with a studied, provocative walk.

Jane Buchanan sighed. "I hope she doesn't take her disappointment out on her horse and run him into the ground on the way home. Josh won't like it."

Amanda's own love for horses was immediately aroused. "Is that likely? I mean—she has been raised on them, hasn't she?" She thought Cathrene was a daughter of one of the other ranchers in the valley. Perhaps this Josh—Cathrene obviously lived within riding distance and was a frequent visitor.

Jane Buchanan made a sound of disgust. "She's not from Owens Valley. She was born and raised in Los Angeles, and she wants to be an actress." Jane Buchanan said *actress* in the same tone of voice she might have said *rattlesnake.* "She's acted in a few movies, but mainly she supports herself by working summers on my brother's ranch. Josh couldn't do without her. He runs a sort of dude-ranch operation in the summer months and takes in visitors. Cathrene's his mainstay. She organizes trail rides and entertainment for the people so they won't find out living on a ranch is nothing but a lot of backbreaking, dust-eating hard work." Jane stared past Amanda to the purple mountains that were visible from the windows. "I

110

suppose we'd have to do the same if Arthur hadn't had his business interests and trained Reid to carry them on."

The affluence of the ranch was apparent to Amanda as she began to prepare the evening meal. The steaks she took from the refrigerator scarcely depleted its stores, and she guessed that Reid's mother had him to thank for the modern appliances in the kitchen, everything from a microwave oven to a dishwasher.

She prepared the potatoes in their foil jackets for the oven, while Janie and Susan helped Jane Buchanan set the table for twelve in the informal dining room. There was informal seating for everyone else in the living room in front of the fireplace. The afternoon passed quickly as Amanda made a light lemon mousse for dessert. The potatoes were almost done when she placed the steaks on the heated grill and began to tear lettuce for the tossed salad.

Janie wandered into the kitchen to watch. Amanda had gotten acquainted with the little girl at lunchtime and liked her at once, although she thought her far too thin and intense for a youngster of her age with miles of countryside to play in. Janie crawled up on the tall wooden stool and sat watching with large brown eyes as Amanda's knife flashed expertly, separating the tomatoes into sections.

"How old were you when you learned to do that?" the girl asked.

"I don't remember," Amanda said, smiling. "I've been cooking for so long I've forgotten when I started. Would you like to try?"

She proferred the knife to Janie, and the girl nodded and slipped off the stool to drag it closer to the counter. Gingerly, she picked up the knife. "Hold it away from you and spear the tomato first," Amanda instructed. "That way you don't squash the insides just trying to break through the skin. Now, start slicing right where you speared it."

There was a commotion in the yard and the repeated bawl of protesting cattle. But Janie ignored it and held her tongue between her newly adult front teeth in such intent concentration that Amanda smiled. "Like this?"

Intent on their task, their heads bent over the counter, neither girl heard the sound of the back door opening and closing. Amanda nodded her approval. "Yes, that's right. You're doing very well." Janie's face glowed with pleasure at Amanda's praise.

"She isn't the only one who is doing very well." Both girls turned startled eyes to the doorway to see Reid Buchanan leaning against its frame, the dust of the range covering his denim jeans and shirt, a red handkerchief hanging around his throat, his hair ruffled from the wind. There was a potent masculinity about him that made Amanda glad for the presence of Janie.

The little girl looked up at him. "I'm helping."

"So I see." He sniffed the air appreciatively. "It smells good. Is everything ready?"

"Yes," Amanda said coolly, glancing at the steaks sizzling on the grill. She resisted the urge to tuck the stray curl at her temple back into her bun. "We're just finishing the salad."

"The men are washing up in the bunk house," Reid said. "Charlie's looking forward to eating someone else's cooking for a change."

Amanda frowned. "Charlie?"

"The range cook," Reid said, and laughed at the look Amanda gave him. "Don't worry. Charlie won't find fault."

112

No one did. They had nothing but compliments for Amanda and her cooking. The men filed into the kitchen, and Amanda filled their plates from the grill while they jostled each other and told Amanda she was prettier than Charlie and asked if she didn't want to take up permanent residence in Owens Valley and be their new cook. Amanda told them she was probably a fool not to take up the sterling offer of slaving over a hot stove on the back of a pickup truck eighteen hours a day, but that she had this boring job in New York she was committed to. Her face was flushed and smiling as she served the last man before Reid Buchanan stepped forward. "Perhaps the boys have the right idea."

"Wait until you've eaten," she said, handing him his plate. "You may change your mind." Forgetting for a moment who he was, she smiled up into his eyes, her face flushed from the men's praise and the knowledge that the meal was a success.

He stood looking down at her, his silvery gaze almost a physical touch as it wandered over her cheeks and down the curve of her throat to linger at the shadowed hollow of her breasts.

"I won't change my mind," he said huskily, the words causing a tingling sensation along her spine. "It looks . . . delicious."

There was a low and insidious curling in her stomach. He was seducing her with his eyes and words. It was subtle and clever, so clever that she couldn't protest. For if she did, it would be tantamount to a confession of her own response.

"I'm glad you think so," she said coolly, as if they were only speaking of the food and turned back to the grill.

113

"Fill your plate and come sit with me, Amanda," he ordered her softly.

"No." Her voice, too, was soft. "I have to serve your mother and Janie—"

"They can take care of themselves. You've been out here long enough."

Jane Buchanan bustled into the kitchen. The tense atmosphere must have been apparent to her. "Amanda, get yourself a plate. Reid, why are you standing there letting your food get cold? Go sit down and eat."

"I'm waiting for Amanda," Reid said calmly. Amanda gritted her teeth. He had purposely enlisted his mother's help, and the older woman didn't disappoint him.

She fastened those feminine gray eyes on Amanda and said, "Well, go on then, child, go eat and relax. You've done enough. And don't worry about the dishes. Susan and David can handle them."

Amanda half expected Reid to protest that, but he said nothing and stood lazily leaning against the doorway, waiting for her.

Mother and son. They were a pair, Amanda thought with exasperation, so accustomed to command that they calmly expected people to obey them without question. She picked up a warm plate and filled it, walking past Reid with her head high, knowing that eating anywhere close to him would be far too disturbing.

In the living room, every chair was full. Men were holding their plates, eating. She stood in the doorway, not quite knowing what to do. From his place on the couch next to David, Bob Conroy made an effort to get to his feet.

"Don't bother, Conroy," a cool voice said behind her. "There's room on the hearth for us."

With a hand on her elbow she wanted to shrug off but couldn't because of the plate she held, she was led to the raised stone hearth. She sat down next to Josh Needham, Jane's brother. Reid settled on the other side of her, far too close, balancing his plate on a dark-trousered thigh that brushed hers. He had showered and changed and wore a silk shirt, midnight blue and western cut. He smelled of that same musky scent she remembered from the day she had worn his robe. It had imprinted itself on her brain and now summoned up a host of unwanted thoughts. She tensed, trying to edge away from him, trying to avoid that brushing contact with his leg. His slight smile told her he knew exactly what she was doing. She bent her head and concentrated on her food, determined to ignore him.

Jane followed them and Bob Conroy rose once more, this time succeeding in offering her his place. She took it, and Bob folded his long legs to sit on the floor next to her and rest his back against the edge of the couch.

Josh, used to eating on the range and on the run, was already finished. He set his plate down on the floor and tugged at the Bull Durham string that hung from his pocket to bring out a bag of tobacco. He fished a cigarette paper out of the other pocket and proceeded to tap the tobacco along its length. When he finished, he tugged the string with his teeth to close the bag. Josh Needham was considerably older than Jane, Amanda guessed, and never married. His nephews were the family he had never had.

"When's the wedding, Davey?" he asked, a twinkle in his eyes. He rolled the cigarette up with one brown hand and ran his tongue along its length.

David lifted his head and smiled at Susan. "We think at the end of this month," he told his uncle. "Susan wants to be a June bride. I'm going to take her in to see the church in Olancha tomorrow. Then she can decide if she wants to be married there or in the city." He grinned. "Once she sees it, I don't think there'll be any question, but I like her to think she's making up her own mind."

Josh grinned. Susan said to her sister, "David says the church is beautiful, Amanda. It has one whole wall of glass that looks out at the mountains. I can't wait to see it."

David continued, "And, of course, with our being married there, Mother will be able to come."

"Of course," Jane Buchanan said stoutly. "I wouldn't miss it for the world."

"Mother," Reid protested, his voice low and intense. "You know the doctor said you should be careful."

"Yes, I know the doctor said I should be careful," she responded tartly. "I hear it often enough. But he didn't say I had to stay in the house and wrap myself in cotton wool. Stop mothering me, Reid."

His mouth quirked. "Someone has to."

"I know what I can and can't do," she said with vigor, "and as my *eldest* son has no intention of marrying and presenting me with a grandchild to hold, I'm certainly going to be present at the wedding of my youngest!"

Reid cut his steak with deft, precise movements and made no reply. David laughed heartily. "Mother, you never change. You know exactly where to hit and how hard."

"I don't think of it that way," Jane said, smiling. She was like her son in that, Amanda thought ruefully.

"I haven't been exactly uncreative," Reid said, his eyes gleaming with amusement. He set his plate on the floor as if to give his mother more of his attention. "The business has experienced a growth ratio of eleven percent since I took over."

"I'm not impressed with your financial empire," his mother said crisply. "The whole thing could fall like a pack of cards tomorrow." She turned her head to look out the long row of windows at the end of the room. Apple trees grew away from the house in orderly rows, the remnants of blossoms still drifting from their boughs. "Children are a permanent contribution to the future. Every spring," she said, nodding toward the trees, "I watch those branches bloom again with new life." Her eyes returned to Reid, moving over his lazily relaxed form. "And every spring I wonder if I'm going to live long enough to see my grandchildren climbing those trees to pick green apples and eat themselves sick, just as my children used to do."

Color flooded Susan's face. David glanced at her. "Mother, you're embarrassing Susan," he said, his voice tinged with amusement.

"Am I?" Jane Buchanan's keen glance raked over the girl. "I didn't think that was possible these days. Young people today know babies aren't brought by the stork." Her eyes twinkled as she looked at her future daughter-in-law. "I certainly did. I was raised on this ranch. When I was about Janie's age, I sat up with my father all night while he tried to help a young mare deliver a foal." The older woman's eyes studied the delicate color that still lingered in Susan's cheeks. "I knew babies didn't come easy. Nothing worthwhile does." She paused and then glanced around the room. Everyone was quiet, listening. "I hope I haven't embarrassed you by speaking frankly, Susan," she said, her voice losing its intense emotional tone, "but when you get to be my age, you feel free to say

117

the things you feel. You suddenly realize that most of what the human race admires is balderdash. There are only two things worthwhile in this world—loving someone and leaving children to carry a part of yourself into the future. Look at Josh there. He hasn't got chick or child. No girl was good enough for him when he was younger, and now no one would have him. All he's got left is a bunch of bawling cattle." A smile curved Jane's lips, taking the sting from her words. Josh studied her with an injured air that was patently exaggerated.

"What you say may be true, Jane," he said slowly. "I'm a bachelor and bound to die one. But that big executive son of yours—" He squinted at Reid, who sat with his back against the fireplace, a slight smile playing around his lips. "Maybe we ought to remind him what happens when a younger sibling gets married before an older one does." His eyes narrowed. "Do you remember, Reid?"

"No, Josh," Reid drawled, leaning forward to watch him from the other side of Amanda. "I don't."

Josh held his cigarette away to study the tip. "You gotta dance in the horse trough."

David exploded into a shout of laughter, and Bob Conroy's face was wreathed in delight. Josh's mouth spread in a sly grin. Reid refused to be drawn.

"Doesn't sound like something I could do too well, Josh."

"That's all right, son," the older man said with mock sympathy. "I didn't think I could, either. But I got lots of help." His eyes swung to Bob Conroy. "There might be a few around here who'd be willing to help you, too." He glanced obliquely at David, who grinned and nodded. "Yes, Reid Buchanan, there'd be a few right willing to help you." Bob Conroy lowered his plate to the floor.

Amanda had a sudden mental picture of them tossing Reid into the large watering trough that stood just outside the south door of the stable.

"I wouldn't try it, Uncle," Reid said, his smile lazy, his voice dry.

Josh's eyes flickered over Amanda. "There's only one way to avoid it," he said slyly.

"Oh?" Reid lifted an eyebrow.

"Grab the nearest female and get her to the altar. I read about you in the paper almost every day with those fancy women you take out. Wouldn't one of them marry you?"

"No doubt," Reid replied with equanimity, "but the feelings weren't mutual."

"Well, then." Josh turned suddenly and his smile at Amanda was predatory. "What about this one? She's sure proved she can cook. And she's pretty enough. Far as I can tell, she'd do to ride the river with." Josh laughed then and there was a murmur of amused sound around the room. Amanda kept her smile firmly on her face to show that she knew it was all teasing. Bob Conroy frowned darkly.

Reid turned his head to study her. She bore his scrutiny with her head raised, her cheeks only faintly suffused with color. "This one might just lead me into some treacherous rapids in that river, Josh," was his amused reply.

It was all lighthearted, of course, but Amanda knew it was also a clear warning that she shouldn't harbor any mistaken ideas about him just because he'd kissed her. She longed to tell him she didn't think she'd ever want to marry him either, but Josh laughed again and slapped his thigh and Amanda had to grab at her plate to save it from sliding to a messy heap on the floor.

"You're a slippery fish just like me, aren't you, son?"

He was still chuckling when Reid said, "How's your calf crop look this year, Josh?"

The older man gave him a keen glance and said, "Best it's been in four years. Got a bunch of real healthy ones this time. The mild spring helped like everything. But we gotta pray for rain as usual. Gotta have enough for us and those city folks, too." He tossed his cigarette into the fireplace. "I should have got out twenty years ago when everyone else did."

Reid smiled. "You'll never leave Owens Valley unless they carry you out. You're too damned stubborn. You love living on the wrong side of the mountains and complaining about it. You know water's always been scarce here."

Josh Needham chuckled. "Not near as stubborn as your ma. She could have lived anywhere in the world she damned well pleased. So what did she do after her husband died? Came back here as fast as she could, that's what she did. Gets in your blood, this living between desert and the smell of mountain pine."

"There are things that get in a man's blood, all right," Reid agreed, and Amanda wondered if he meant the valley.

"Well, I'm glad Owens Valley isn't in mine," David said with a laugh. "Freeze in the winter, sweat in the summer, and smell of cattle and horses all year round. That's not my idea of paradise. I'm just glad Dad had enough sense to build his empire in companies instead of cattle." He grinned at Susan. "I'm a city boy, and I've found me a city girl."

"Which brings us back to your brother," Josh Needham said, a sudden sly note in his voice as he rose to his feet.

"You and I got a date, Reid Buchanan. With a horse trough."

A sinewed arm snaked out, grasping Reid and hauling him to his feet. Normally, there would have been no contest between the two men for Reid was stronger and younger, but he had been caught off guard, and now Bob Conroy was on his feet and rushing to join the fray. David, too, had risen and entered the struggle. The three of them had no success in pinning Reid's arms or controlling him until a high-heeled boot caught Amanda's shin and she cried out in pain and surprise. Reid's hard muscles relaxed at once and he twisted his head to look at her. "Amanda?" he said. That was his downfall. That moment of nonresistance was all the other three needed. With a concerted effort, they dragged him to the front door and thrust him through it. Amanda sat staring after them for a moment, feeling sick and guilty. She knew that the wrestling was being done in fun, but she knew too that it would have been all over by now if it hadn't been for her cry of pain. The three men would never have succeeded in carrying Reid outside if he hadn't tried to see about her. Now there was a chance someone would be hurt, perhaps accidentally, and she was to blame.

She sprang to her feet and ran to the door with a hazy idea of stopping them somehow. Susan and Janie, as well as a half dozen of the other cowboys who guessed something was up, followed her. Outside, the soft air of the twilight evening was heavy with sound—the bawling of cattle and the rustle of cottonwood leaves. The air was cool and felt like fine silk against the skin.

Amanda ran toward the stable. As she rounded the corner, her heart was pounding. The gate of the corral was open, and she was six feet from the concrete trough when

121

out of the melee Reid, held spread-eagled, was lifted and dropped with a resounding splash into the tank of water. Her stomach heaved. Oh, God, what if he hit his head against the concrete or he twisted a leg under him as he went down. . . . Blood seemed to pound in her brain, and breathing was impossible. Then she heard boisterous laughter and raucous calling, and she saw Reid get to his feet and stand, dripping with water, staring at his uncle from the middle of the trough. His shirt was soaked and clung to his torso, and water streamed down his face from his hair. He shoved the wet strands back with an impatient hand and swung a leg over the side of the tank. An exquisite relief bubbled through Amanda and ended in the escape of a nervous little laugh from her throat.

Reid turned his head and stared at her. Then his eyes glinted, and his smile was pure menace. He began to walk toward her, his boots sloshing, his clothes dripping water with every step. He looked so ridiculous and so human, so unlike the fierce executive that she had first met, that she dissolved into helpless laughter. The crowd did, too. "Do you find me amusing, Amanda Kirk?" Reid growled softly.

"I'm sorry," she said, holding her hands in front of her and backing away as he continued relentlessly toward her. "I couldn't help it—"

He never broke his stride. He was openly stalking her now, and she was holding her hands in front of her and backing away as best she could. "Josh," Reid called to his uncle, who stood behind him, grinning, his shirt wet. "Amanda's older than her sister." His eyes never left Amanda's laughing face.

Josh grinned even wider. "Is she now? She ought to do a little dancing, too, then."

122

Amanda moved back and Reid moved forward. "Don't, please," she pleaded. "I'm sorry. I didn't mean to laugh at you." She looked into his mock menacing face, heard the squishing of his boots, and dissolved into helpless laughter all over again. It was her undoing. Reid captured her with hard, wet hands and swung her off the ground into the cradle of his arms. He swung around and headed back to the tank, his steps relentless, his clothes cold and wet against her. She kicked her feet in the air, alternately laughing and pleading. "Reid, don't, please. I'm sorry—"

They were almost back to the tank. She could feel his stride slowing to compensate for the slick, wet ground. Moisture seeped through her clothes from his. She resigned herself to her fate, thinking she couldn't get much wetter, when from the stunned crowd a small figure ran and threw itself at Reid.

"You put her down! Don't you throw her in the water. She's my friend." Janie clung to Reid's thigh like a leech. "Put her down," she cried.

Reid looked down into the fierce little face and then back at Amanda. "You're lucky to have a champion." He still held Amanda over the water threateningly. "I wasn't so lucky." He held her in his arms for what seemed like an eternity, looking down at her. She laughed back at him, her eyes alight with a reckless bravado, daring him to do his worst. She no longer cared whether he dropped her into the water or not. There was a breathless silence in the watching crowd as they sensed a decision being made, one they were powerless to stop or alter. Then, abruptly, Reid swung her away from the water and lowered her feet to the ground. He didn't let her go. He held her against him, his eyes dark and brooding, sweeping over her upturned face. She smelled the scent of him and felt his lean, wet body against her, and something so strong, so real, so intense seemed to flame up between them that she was frightened by its power. She shivered instinctively.

The man who held her turned into a polite stranger and stepped away. "I've made you wet," he said. "You'd better go change before you catch pneumonia."

The laughter died in her eyes. She searched his face for a hint of the cause of his chilly withdrawal. She felt a small hand touching hers.

"Are you all right?"

Distracted, she looked down at Janie. "I'm fine, darling."

"He made you all wet," Janie declared, looking at the dark spots on Amanda's blouse and pants.

Jane Buchanan emerged from the crowd and took Janie by the hand. "Come along, it's time you were in bed, little one. Reid, for heaven's sake, sometimes I think you men will never grow up. Amanda, go change and get right into bed." She continued to scold and worry the crowd until everyone began to walk away.

Inside Reid's room, Amanda closed the door and leaned against it. She felt shivery and cold. She pressed her hand against her stomach to relieve the ache there, and the touch of her wet clothes against her fingers reminded her that she had to get out of them. There was a bath adjacent to Reid's bedroom and she stepped into it, peeled off her damp things, and got into the shower. She turned the water on high and hot and let it pour over her, blanking everything out of her mind but its sensual touch.

It was only a short respite. Thoughts poured through her the minute she stepped out and stood drying herself with a fluffy towel. She slipped into her nightgown and sat down on the bed, no longer able to keep her thoughts at bay. Her mind replayed everything through in scrupulous detail. But it was not what had happened that was hard to understand. The whole thing had been nothing more than a harmless bit of horseplay. It was her own reactions that were so frightening. Right from the beginning, she had wanted it to stop. And why? *Why?* The truth clamored at her mind, but she couldn't face it. Restlessly, she got up and went to the dresser to take down her hair. A stranger stared back at her from the mirror, a stranger with wide green eyes and flowing hair, a vulnerable, defenseless stranger. She turned away from the mirror and went back to the bed and sat down, shivering, hugging herself. "No," she whispered softly. "No."

Slowly, relentlessly the truth seeped into her mind like sand through the narrow neck of an hourglass. She had been afraid for Reid. She had gone racing out into the yard in an attempt to protect him, probably the strongest and fittest man of them all. When she saw that powerful body falling, her heart had almost stopped beating. But then, later, when she herself had been threatened with a dunking— She moaned and buried her head in her hands. She hadn't cared at all. In his arms, she could have faced anything. He could have dangled her from the edge of a cliff over a mile-deep chasm and she would have felt the same reckless joy, the same wild surge of happiness at being in his arms. She knew that at that instant she would have trusted him with her life. Oh, God, she had no reason to, no reason at all. He had undermined her father and nearly ruined her sister's chances for a happy marriage. He was ruthless and unfeeling, she reminded herself fiercely, a man who headed a giant corporation—one that swallowed up other companies and rearranged people's lives and careers without a second thought. But, somehow, she couldn't remember that man. She had discovered another one, a man whose arms around her felt secure and right. The memory of those few moments in his arms made a surge of warmth like heady wine flood through every inch of her body.

It wasn't logical. Was this . . . this trust as stupidly capricious as love? Did it come from his physical strength, the superb form and condition of his male body? She knew that wasn't so. She had been held in his arms. His power had been complete over her. She should have been afraid, or at the very least, angry. But she hadn't been. She had been utterly sure that whether Reid dropped her or held her, she wouldn't have been hurt. He would have kept her safe. She would have trusted him with her life. *And he was the man she had come to manipulate!* For her father's sake, true. But, nevertheless . . .

Her skin prickled with cold. She crawled into bed and lay there, staring up into the dark. The apple trees outside her window creaked gently in the spring breeze; the boughs moved, tracing dark fingers of shadow across her ceiling. Oh, how had it happened? How had Reid broken down the barrier she had erected after Colin? She barely knew Reid. Yet he had stormed her castle, not with his strength, but with his vulnerability, with a sensitivity she had never imagined he could possess. He could have flattened his uncle with one stroke this afternoon, she thought. He had dealt with Colin in half the time. He could have laughed at Janie and dumped Amanda into the water and walked away, disregarding a small girl's distress as childish, knowing Amanda would not be the worse for a wetting. But he hadn't. He had responded to a little girl and let Amanda go.

Now she wasn't free at all.

She lay there, listening to the night sounds, the rustle of the cottonwood leaves, the occasional bawl of a cow. It was cool in the room, but perspiration made her silk gown cling to her skin. She tossed restlessly under the covers. The house was quiet. She couldn't close her eyes. Sleep was unthinkable. She was caught, caught between a rock as hard as Half Dome's sliced granite wall and a place as demanding as Death Valley.

And all because Reid Buchanan was not the hard, unfeeling executive she had thought he was. He was a sensitive man who cared about people's feelings—Josh's, Janie's . . . and her own. And even—if she was totally honest—her father's.

Unbidden, the bleak tone of Reid's voice came back to her. "I suppose you wouldn't believe me if I told you I had your father's best interest in mind. . . ." She hadn't believed it then. But now she wasn't so sure. That quick, incisive mind could cut to the heart of any problem and then consider it from every angle.

The moon rose over the mountains, painting the ghostly outline of apple leaves and branches on her wall with a feather brush of light and shadow. She stared, fascinated at the twisting, writhing shapes that danced across the room. Her life was like that, she thought, twisted and caught between the lifelong loyalty she felt for her father and the new, surprising trust she had in Reid. What could she do? Her father depended on her to help him. But Reid . . . Reid was a cynical man whose experience with women had left him in need, too. He needed to be shown that not all women were dishonest gold diggers who thought only of themselves. She sat up and punched her pillow. Changing Reid Buchanan's attitude was a large order and one she probably couldn't fill. And she couldn't let her father down.

She lay back, grimacing. But if she told Reid the truth, openly, bluntly, as she longed to do, what would his reaction be? She sighed. She was probably agonizing for nothing. There was a good possibility he had already guessed her reason for coming with Susan this weekend. She would just have to tell him the truth and take the consequences, whatever they might be. After that, she would return to New York. There was nothing else she could do.

Her decision made, she closed her eyes, sure now that she could sleep. She couldn't. What would his reaction to her frankness be? She didn't dare to think. She tossed for another hour and then got up and slipped into her wrap. It was lightweight for night prowling, but it was all she had. It really made no difference; everyone was in bed. She had seen a box of cocoa mix in the cabinet that afternoon. She would make herself a hot drink. Anything was better than lying there with her own restless mind.

It wasn't till she got to the end of the hall that she saw the light. Someone was still up. She knew with heart-pounding certainty whose low voice it was she heard, sounding as if he spoke on the telephone.

She tugged the tie tighter around her waist and walked forward, seeing Reid's dark head bathed in a pool of light. He was bent over the telephone on the stand next to the couch, and he scribbled on a yellow legal-sized pad he held in his lap. Her heart began to pound. If he went on talking and didn't look up, she could slip by him.

"—need that cost sheet from that Nevada copper mine by Monday, Tom."

She walked past him, a ghost in pale satin at the edge of the shadows. His sixth sense must have warned him.

"Hang on a minute," he said into the receiver. He looked up, straining to see beyond the light. "Who is it?"

His tone was sharp, demanding, and she knew she had to turn and identify herself. "It's me, Amanda. I'm sorry if I disturbed you." His eyes narrowed, focusing on her with difficulty. "I was going to make myself some cocoa," she said lamely. "I didn't know anyone was still up."

"Couldn't you sleep?" The question was blunt.

She shook her head. He was the one who should be in bed, she thought. He had showered and changed since his dunking and wore jeans and a knit shirt, but his eyes drooped with fatigue and there were lines of strain around his mouth. His dark hair was disheveled, his jaw dark with late-night beard. He looked alone and vulnerable and very weary.

"Could . . . could I get you some?" she heard herself asking.

"Yes." He stared at her. "Yes, I could use some." He glanced down at the receiver impatiently. "What? Look, Tom, this can't wait. I've got to have that—"

His attention was diverted, and Amanda escaped to the kitchen. She closed the door and flicked on the light. The gleaming matter-of-factness of the yellow appliances and wood cabinets reassured her. She felt comfortable here. No reason why she shouldn't, she had spent most of her day in this room. She moved around easily, setting the kettle to boil and emptying the envelopes of powder into two cups. When the water was hot, she poured it over the chocolate and stirred both cups before putting them on a tray and carrying them through to the living room.

Reid sat where she had left him, but now his dark head was laid back against the plaid cushion and his eyes were closed. He must have fallen asleep the moment he had finished his conversation. It wasn't surprising, really. He could hardly work like a cowboy all day and play the executive all night without feeling the strain.

She put the tray on the low table and reached down to take her cup and go to her room when a tanned hand closed around her wrist. "Were you planning on leaving me?"

The low, husky tone seemed to vibrate against her nerves. "I thought you were asleep."

"Since you aren't, sit down. Keep me company."

She hesitated. "You're working . . ."

"Not now." He let go of her wrist and flung the pad on the floor. "I'm through for the night, I guess. Everyone I need to talk to is sick in bed. This damn flu must be of epidemic proportions." He leaned back and laced his fingers through his hair.

"And that's where you'll be, if you don't get some sleep," Amanda said coolly, walking around and sitting down on the couch a comfortable distance away. She picked her cup up and warmed her palms with it. "Sick in bed just like everyone else."

"If there's one thing I can always depend on arousing in you," he said softly, "it's your maternal instinct." He closed his eyes. His lashes lay long and dark against his skin, his mouth relaxed, curved into a half smile.

She gazed at him, her throat closing. She hardly felt maternal with him.

"Were you that way with Brent?" he asked, keeping his eyes closed, as if he were too weary to open them. "Maternal?"

The name was obtrusive, unwelcome. The words were spoken softly, though without the sting that usually lay in his tone when he spoke of Colin.

"I must have been," she said ruefully, her words ending in a soft, deprecatory laugh. She had never felt anything like this for Colin. God, nothing like this!

"There are worse things." His dark-lashed lids were still covering his eyes, and she was thankful for that. If he had opened his eyes at this moment, he would have seen the desire flaring boldly in hers.

"It wasn't what Colin wanted," she murmured, amazed to hear how cool her voice sounded, as if it belonged to another woman, not the one who sat there devouring him with her eyes, watching that male mouth soften, its upper lip curving ever so slightly, its sensual lower one making her ache to touch it with her fingertip and then lean forward and take it gently in her teeth.

"Brent is a fool," Reid murmured, unmoving.

"You've said that before," she said softly, holding her breath. His breathing deepened and slowed. She went on watching him. His body was stretched out almost flat on the cushions, his muscular legs extended to their full length in the jeans. The tan knit shirt strained over his muscled chest and left a deep V of dark hair bare at his throat. This man was stunningly attractive—primitive and real—and far more dangerous to her than the angry executive who had stormed out of his office in San Francisco.

Her hands shook, and she realized she was still holding the cup of cocoa. It had become cold and was congealing on top. She leaned forward to place the cup on the tray when something moved. She stilled her body, thinking she had wakened Reid, and turned to look at him. He had not moved. He was deeply asleep. She must have imagined she felt him moving beside her. Or had she hoped he was?

She stared at him, knowing that tomorrow she would

have to tell him her reason for coming to the ranch, but tonight . . . tonight she wanted to kiss him. She wanted to feel her mouth against his own, to savor the taste of him. She had wanted it since this afternoon. Rising up from some primitive place deep inside, the urge had nothing to do with conscious thought. She simply wanted to pretend for a moment that she belonged to him and he belonged to her.

His eyes remained closed, his breathing deep and even. He was asleep. The temptation was overpowering. A strange and wanton impulse guiding her, she leaned forward, supporting herself with her hands on the cushion on either side of him. Carefully, she brushed her lips over his, allowing her mouth to linger there for just an instant. Her heart pounding, she drew away at once, watching him. He neither woke nor stirred. She sat utterly still. Had she hoped he would wake and take her in his arms and return her kiss? She didn't know the answer to that. She might desire him, but how foolish it would be to hope that he might care for her! The mountain air must be getting to her. She wasn't a glamorous model or an actress. It would be disastrous to become involved with Reid Buchanan.

She tensed her muscles to force herself to leave and stood up. She leaned over, reaching for the tray, when she was grasped by the waist and pulled down into his lap, held by the steel grip of his arms, cradled against him, his fingers resting lightly on her mouth to restrain any sound she might make.

She stared up into the dark, slumberous eyes, which gazed down at her with amused satisfaction, and knew they were too alert to belong to a man who had suddenly wakened.

"You weren't asleep at all," she sputtered, too annoyed

at being fooled to fully register the fact that she was in his arms in the dark quiet of the house.

"I must have been," he murmured, gazing down at her, his eyes glittering with laughter. "I dreamed you were kissing me."

CHAPTER 7

"I . . . I felt sorry for you," she said. "You looked tired and I—" She struggled, trying to sit up. He restrained her, holding her close to his chest with ease. "The maternal instinct at work again," he murmured. His eyes traveled slowly over her flame-colored hair, which lay against pale gown and skin. With lazy carelessness, he drew one finger down the neckline of her wrap, tracing the gentle curve of her breast down to the depth of the valley and making his erotic way up the other side. "In this gown, you don't look maternal. You look like a tantalizing goddess who wears clothes the color of her skin to drive men mad."

She was powerless to move. It was all she could do to battle her own languorous need to lie back in his arms and shiver with delight under his seductive caress. "Reid, don't—"

"Amanda, don't," he said mockingly, his eyes gleaming over her. "Don't make your token protest." His mouth touched her cheek lightly. His words seemed to be entering her brain directly through her skin. "Kiss me again, Amanda. Now, when I'm a willing participant."

His lips tantalized her mouth, hovering just above it. Unable to tolerate the anticipation, she slid her arms around his neck. A soft moan came from her throat as she brought his mouth to hers. Reid let her keep the initiative, let her explore the line of his upper lip, but when she took his lower one gently between her teeth, he groaned and caught her to him. He took her mouth with a possessiveness that was expert and complete, parting her lips to explore the sweetness of her mouth, sending shock waves of need and longing through her like a depth charge. When she was completely lost, her body demanding total intimate knowledge of him, he took her by the shoulders and held her away. She stared up at him, her pupils wide, her body alive with craving.

"Do you still think I'm Colin, Amanda?"

The name might have belonged to the language of another planet for all it meant to her. She had forgotten that she had lied to him, kept him away with Colin's name. That was the trouble with lies; one tended to forget them. "Reid, I—"

"Don't," he muttered, the word heavy. He pulled her close. "It doesn't matter anymore." He took her mouth again in a soul-destroying kiss, his lips warm on hers, possessing her, claiming her. She did not deny his ownership. She acknowledged it and more, giving of herself freely and fully. She slid her hands under his open shirt, feeling the beat of his heart against them.

"I have to go to London tomorrow," he said. "Don't go back to the city, Amanda. Stay here with my mother."

"No," she said, thinking only of how she would miss him. "Take me with you."

He gathered her into his arms. "I'd like nothing better, but you'd be far too much of a distraction." He held her, smoothing back a lock of red-gold hair. "Marry me, Amanda. Have my children."

"What?" Holding his arm, she pulled herself upright in his lap. "Reid, I . . . I haven't known you very long."

"But we've gotten acquainted very quickly," he said, a faint smile touching his mouth.

Color crept up her throat and into her cheeks. She struggled to get away from him. He allowed her to stand up, his only attempt to stop her a caressive hand sliding from hip to thigh, a caress that almost destroyed her resolve to move away.

"I don't know," she said, shaking her head, lifting a hand to smooth her tousled hair. She took a step away from his disturbing closeness so she could think. "I need more time."

"Do you?" He rose and put his hands on her shoulders, turning her toward him. His hands were warm through her wrap. "A moment ago, you didn't." She buried her flushed face against his chest, giving in to his tender touch and the warm, remembered smell of him. Gently, he tilted her face up to his. "Say yes, Amanda."

"I'm . . . I'm afraid," she said, whispering the truth, unable to hold it back. "What will everyone think? My father, your mother?"

He pulled her close, his hand stroking her nape under the heavy mass of hair. "Do you remember the reason I told you Susan and David shouldn't wait?"

Her cheek, pressed against his bare chest, warmed with color.

"I want you, Amanda. All the time in the world won't change what happens when we touch each other." His lips moved against her temple. "Are you afraid to trust me because of what Brent did?" He held her away to smile down at her. "There will be no long engagement. We'll be married as soon after Susan and David as it can be ar-

136

ranged. Until then, I want you here with my mother where you'll be safe. You can ride and get a suntan and relax."

"Safe?" A frown creased her forehead.

His smile was warm. "Have you forgotten I'm a rich man, darling, and the target for every gossipmonger and would-be fanatic who dreams of making his fortune by threatening me? You'll be in danger the moment the press learns of our engagement. I want you here with my mother, surrounded by the protection that the boys and Conroy are providing for her."

"I can't stay here, Reid," she argued softly. "I'll have to go back and talk to my father. And I'll have to go to New York and tell Milton I'm giving up my job."

"I'll speak to your father, and we'll go to New York together, this week after I come back from London." He traced a finger lightly over her face. "Will your father get over his hatred of me, do you think?"

She lifted liquid green eyes to him. "He'll have to, won't he? Because you're going to be the father of his grandchildren."

His kiss was fierce and left her trembling with desire. "How in hell am I supposed to leave you when you say things like that," he muttered when he lifted his head.

She stared up into his dark face and then reached around him to turn off the lamp, plunging the room into darkness. Only the moonlight streaming through the window gave the room any light at all. "Reid," she whispered, her voice full of aching longing. "Don't leave me, tonight. Please."

A shred of moonlight warmed the dark silver glitter of his eyes. For a long moment he stood looking down at her. "Reid," she said again, burying her lips in the hair-crisped flesh of his chest, driven by a wild, irrational need of him, a need that ate into her like a liquid fire.

His hands were harsh on her shoulders. He held her away, but not far, as if he could only bear to have her a little way from him. "Dammit, Amanda, I—"

She shivered with humiliation and an emptiness that was almost intolerable. She stepped out of his arms and stood facing the window, her body in the satin wrap outlined in the moonlight. She clenched her hands, fighting her need, aware of him silently watching her from behind. For what seemed like endless moments, she stood there, facing away from him, praying he would make some move toward her.

"You unholy witch," he murmured from behind, his hands moving in front of her, cupping her breasts, pulling her back against him, sending a surge of wild relief through her. "Do you have any idea how you look, standing there in the moonlight like a pale goddess with fiery hair?" He buried his face in its silken depths at the side of her neck.

She turned in his arms. Here she felt whole. She felt caught, yet she was free. She soared, yet couldn't leave. It was everything she had felt in his arms before. But this was better. She had the freedom to kiss and touch him. Her hands moved over the hard back, discovering each muscle and bone. She arched her body against his in silent offering, saying with her lips and hands what she couldn't say in words.

For a long moment, he allowed her to explore him with her hands, her mouth. Then he turned her to walk beside him. When she realized where he was going, reality intruded. Her heart pounded, her knees felt weak. Reid was opening the bedroom door. There was no going back. She had invited him to make love to her, and he had accepted her invitation. Butterflies battered against her stomach. Suppose she didn't satisfy him? He was worldly, experienced.

A gentle hand at the back of her waist moved her into the room, and the door closed softly behind her. The apple trees creaked gently in the wind. Their shadows played across the walls. A surge of panic rose within her. "Reid, I—"

"No," he murmured softly. "There's no going back, darling, not now."

He turned her toward him and nestled one finger in the soft spot at the base of her throat. Slowly, he let it wander lower, over her skin down between her breasts to the tie at her waist. With one quick movement, the tie was loose and her wrap was open. Hard hands at her shoulders let the silky garment slide to the floor. She shivered and clung to him. The cut of her gown made it a simple matter for those same warm hands to slide it off her shoulders and down her body. His hands smoothed it over the silky length of her, brushing her arms, hips, and thighs with the fire of his caress as they moved downward. When the gown lay at her feet, she was pressed back into the warm bed that she had left only moments ago. Reid's bed, the bed he had slept in as a child. But he was no longer a child. In the moonlight, a man was emerging, a man of bone and muscle and sinew.

His lean form stretched beside her, and a warm hand found the sensitive underside of her jaw. He traced the bones of her face. "Do you have any idea how beautiful you are at this moment, Amanda? Soft, feminine, and loving . . ."

He moved to kiss her, his hard chest nudging her breast.

139

His mouth covered hers, and his tongue probed gently, flicking over the top of hers, discovering the sweetness of her slowly and with great tenderness. His hand circled the swollen warmth of her breast. She gasped with pleasure. His other hand was underneath her, probing to find the erogenous spot at the small of her back. Then his mouth left hers and sought the dark peak of her breast, which was ready for him. He teased and caressed it with his tongue, his erotic possession making a soft moan of delight rise from her throat. She buried her hands in the silky hair of his nape and breathed in the clean male scent of him. Her fingers moved down his back, seeking and finding the hard bones, the muscles that moved with silken precision under the sleek skin. He raised his head. Even in the pale light she could see the glitter of desire and possession in the gray depths. "You're an illusion," he murmured. "You can't be real. . . ."

She knew at once what he meant. What they were sharing was so right, so good, that it couldn't be real. "You are the one who is an illusion," she murmured. She placed her palms against his chest and touched the reality of him—the hair-crisped skin, the male nipples, the heart that pulsed steadily against her palm.

With a soft laugh, he imitated her, cupping her breasts in his hands. "Poor Amanda! I'm not nearly as interesting as you are to explore. . . ." He traced a circle around her breasts and wandered up to crest the peak. She laughed softly, glorying in the femininity he was so obviously admiring. Then, in one swift moment, laughter flared into passion. He bent to her and kissed her deeply. His warm lips left hers to travel lower over the sensitive skin of her throat and visit again the peaks and valleys. She was bathed in sensual delight—the feel of his weight against her, the scent of him, the brush of his hair against her skin, the warm seeking of his mouth against her breast. She moaned softly in a wordless plea. His own harsh groan of need answered her, and he moved over her to make her his.

In the aftermath of languor, she slept. When she woke in the morning, he was gone. If it had not been for the tingling remembrance in her body, she would have thought she dreamed it. She rose and dressed in jeans, a plaid shirt, and her riding boots. The night before *must* have been a dream. Reid hadn't asked her to marry him. She must have fantasized it all. And it was only then that she realized that neither of them had spoken a word of love.

Sobered, she tiptoed through the kitchen. Someone had made a pot of coffee, but the thought of it made her stomach lurch. She let herself out of the house and headed across the yard to the stable. She needed consolation. And she had always found that on the back of a horse. She could at least go and look at them.

The brick-colored dirt clung to her tan boots. She climbed the two steps up to the stable door. It was warmer inside the shadowed depths than the morning air had been and smelled of horse and hay and leather. There were only three horses in the stalls, a roan, a palomino, and a mottled gray, a small horse that looked as if it might have been Janie's mount. The roan had dark liquid brown eyes. It joggled the wall of its stall and bobbed its head over the rough boards at her. She reached out a tentative hand to its velvety nose. The horse turned into her palm as if used to the petting, blew softly and nickered low.

"I didn't bring you sugar, darling," Amanda said softly. "It's bad for your teeth, you know. Next time I'll bring you a carrot." She went on crooning to the animal, engrossed in the sensual feel of the horse under her fingers and its warm blowing into her hand until a sound caused her to tense and turn.

Bob Conroy stood behind her, his face shadowed in the light, his slender frame clad in a denim jacket and jeans. "What are you doing here?" His tone wasn't aggressive, but there was a challenging quiet about him.

"Talking to the roan." She turned back to the horse, feeling ill at ease and guilty when she had no reason. "Is that all right?"

"It's all right with me," the young cowboy drawled. "Have you checked with Buchanan?"

She turned away and ran her hand along the roan's muzzle, feeling strangely disturbed by the quiet tone of his voice. "Whose horse is this?" she asked.

"Jane's. She doesn't ride him anymore." There was a pause, then, "Do you ride?"

"Yes. I just learned last year, and I'm hopelessly addicted." She smiled self-consciously. "I suppose that sounds stupid to someone who spends all day in the saddle."

He didn't return her smile. "Where did you learn?"

"Out East. But I've ridden with a Western saddle." The roan bobbed restlessly in the stall. "What . . . what is everyone doing this morning?"

"Sorting the calves."

He folded his arms across his chest and leaned back against the stall next to the roan, facing her. His eyes were a vivid shade of blue. They were fastened on her face. "How long are you planning to stay in Owens Valley?"

"Just for the weekend." Amanda brushed her hand over the velvety nose. The roan snorted and bobbed its head.

142

In the shadowed stable there was a quiet intimacy that disturbed her. "What do you feed the horses?"

"Hay, ground oats." He tilted his head. "The same thing you feed your horses out East," he mocked gently.

She groped for words, somehow needing them to create distance between them. "How long have you worked for Mrs. Buchanan?"

"A couple of seasons."

The succinct answer stopped her efforts to make conversation. Silently, she kept her hand on the roan, taking comfort from the smoothness of the animal's hide under her hand, but there was a stillness about the man who stood there watching her, a waiting, a message of personal interest in his eyes that had nothing to do with their polite conversation. One of the other horses moved restlessly and bumped the wall of its stall. The smell of hay and horse drifted to her nose and she dropped her hand. "Well, I suppose I'd better be getting back to the house."

She turned to go. He moved away from the wall and stepped into her path. "Don't go."

"I—"

"I was watching the house last night," he said slowly. "You shouldn't stand in the window with a light-colored nightgown on."

Color rushed to her cheeks. "You saw me?"

He didn't answer, but his eyes never left her face. "Are you sure you know what you're doing?"

She lifted her chin. "I . . . don't know what you mean."

"You're not his type."

Angered, she said coolly, "What possible business is that of yours?"

He didn't touch her, but there was a coiled watchfulness

143

in the slim, muscled body that told her he would stop her if she tried to walk around him.

"Old Western traditions die hard."

"What old traditions?"

"The old tradition of protecting our wives and sweethearts from predators." He gazed at her.

"I'm not your wife or sweetheart," she said steadily.

"Maybe I'd like you to be." There was a quiet challenge in his words.

"I don't even know you." She couldn't let him believe he could interfere in her life, even if he was attracted to her. But she had to admit there was a quiet strength about him she admired. "I've been taking care of myself for a number of years. I hardly know you, and I don't think I need your help."

"I think you need all the help you can get," he said bluntly.

"Why is that, Conroy?"

She had been intent on Bob, annoyed with him. She had not seen Reid enter the stable. Now Bob half turned toward Reid and his slim body seemed to straighten to its full height. Even so, Reid's aura of power and masculinity dominated the younger man. Amanda's nervous agitation made her aware of everything about Reid, his lean figure clothed in a denim shirt, the fit of his faded jeans, his dark hair tousled by the morning breeze. Reid took the few steps that brought him to Amanda's side with an air of hard purpose and the predatory grace of a male cougar.

"What are you doing here?" he asked Conroy, his voice soft, the steel lying just below the surface. "You're hired to watch the house, not entertain Miss Kirk."

"I'm off duty," Bob said, his voice tight. "It's Tom's shift." His eyes flickered to her. "I followed Amanda in

144

here to make sure she didn't get her head kicked in by a horse."

Reid's eyes sliced over the other man, and Amanda knew he had not missed the fact that Bob had called her by her given name. "That wasn't necessary. She's an accomplished horsewoman."

"So she told me."

A spark of anger flared in Reid's eyes. "Getting acquainted with my fiancée, were you?" he said smoothly.

In the dim light of the stable, Bob Conroy's face seemed to tighten. He turned his head and stared at Amanda. "Is that true?"

"Why should you doubt it?" Reid said coolly before Amanda could answer.

His blue eyes glittering, Conroy turned back to Reid. "Yesterday I helped throw you in the tank because you didn't have a wife."

Reid's lips moved in a mocking smile. "Maybe that's what changed my mind."

"I can't believe that!" The words were harsh and explosive.

"You'd better," Reid said softly.

There was a silence in the stable. One of the horses moved restlessly as if sensing the air of tension.

Then Conroy turned to her, a cool dislike glittering in his eyes. "Is it true?"

"Yes," she said, her voice husky.

His face became remote and cool. "Then I offer you my best wishes, Miss Kirk. Now, if you'll excuse me."

He went out, his back ramrod-straight. The stable was quiet. "I . . . I guess I'll go back to the house—" she said, and took a step to walk by Reid. He caught her arm. "Was he making a pass at you?"

145

His fingers were warm and hard on her bare skin. "We were just talking about the horses." Her green eyes lifted to him. His hand loosened slightly. Curious, she gazed up at him. "Are you going to be a jealous husband?"

Coolly, he said, "Any man is."

The hope that had flared in her died. No, any man wasn't. Not Reid Buchanan, who could have any woman he wanted. She was much more likely to be the jealous wife. Because . . . because if he did take another woman for his mistress, she would care. Dear God, she would care very much!

"Having second thoughts?"

"Perhaps. I—"

"Then we'll dispel them."

He folded her into his arms, and his lips came down with that soul-destroying warmth she was beginning to know well. She seemed to be floating somewhere, rising up on her toes. Her senses were filled with him, the warm, clean smell of his body, the feel of his silky hair under her hands. His mouth left hers to nuzzle her neck. "I like your hair. You look like a child with it tied up in a yellow ribbon that way. I don't blame Conroy for wanting you."

His husky voice made her pulse pound. "What makes you think he wanted me?"

"A man would be a fool not to." His lips explored the hollow of her throat, sending impulses of sensation through her whole body. Desperate to distract him, she said, "I . . . I thought we might go riding this morning."

"So you want to go riding, do you?" There was a husky undertone of amusement in his voice, as if he knew very well why she was asking him to take her riding.

She managed to smile at him. "I think it would be much safer, don't you?"

He chuckled and let her go. "Safer, but not as pleasurable as what I had in mind." His smile was caressive. "I'll saddle the roan for you. My horse is down at the branding corral."

The powerful muscles of his shoulders moved smoothly under the rough blue shirt as he threw the blanket over the roan's back and followed it with the saddle. He fastened the cinch and drew the bridle over the horse's head.

Moments later, she was outside, mounted on the roan, with Reid beside her adjusting her stirrups.

She breathed in deeply. The horse's height gave her the advantage of an unrestricted view beyond Reid's shoulder. Acres of wide blue sky stretched above. Clouds flattened themselves in white streamers over purple mountain peaks. To her left, brown desert hills rose covered with scrub. In front of her, the pines and cottonwoods around the house were a deep green. It was a visual feast, with anything she cared to sample waiting for her at the turn of her head.

The sound of another horse's hooves reached her ears. The black silhouette of a horse and rider approached from the road and galloped toward the ranch house.

"Good morning," the husky voice of Cathrene Taylor called. No one else could have held the reins with such careless grace, such confident assurance of control over a high-spirited Arab stallion. The horse danced sideways, lifting little dust clouds under its shod feet.

Cathrene guided the stallion past Amanda toward the front of the house and got off him, tossing the reins over the rail fence. She walked toward them with that same provocative roll of hip Amanda had noticed the first day she had met the girl.

"Hello, Reid," Cathrene said, walking toward him and ignoring Amanda. "You're up early this morning."

"So are you," Reid said, smiling, his eyes frankly admiring the curves under the brown silk blouse, the smooth riding pants. And why not? Cathrene's eyes were highlighted with a subtle touch, and her mouth was a glossy pink that might have been caused by the action of her tongue. She was a beautiful young woman by anyone's standards, and now smiling up at Reid, her teeth white and even in her tanned face, she sparkled. "Poor darling," she continued, smiling at Reid, then glancing at Amanda astride the horse whose reins Reid still held. "Are you playing ranch host and leading Amanda around the paddock?"

"Not exactly," Reid said, smiling indulgently at the girl. "We were just going to take the roan out for a run." He smiled with genuine amusement, and Amanda almost caught her breath at the charm he exuded. "I'd ask you to come along but—" He nodded toward the stallion. "I get tired of eating that animal's dust. Did you want to see Jane?"

Cathrene shook her head, her dark hair moving against her cheek. "I came to see you and to meet Amanda's sister, David's fianceé. I met Amanda yesterday," she said dismissively.

"I think they're down watching the branding. I'm just on my way to get my horse. I'll walk down with you."

Something hot and clawing flooded Amanda. She said nothing, but with a sour taste at the back of her throat she took full control of the roan and turned him. The stallion, seeing that the other horse was moving, neighed and tossed his head in protest.

Reid turned back. "Go fasten that brute properly, Cath-

148

rene. I've never thought him completely civilized. If he took it in his head to pull loose, you'd never catch him."

Cathrene shrugged her shoulders. "He's okay. He's just restless." She smiled into Reid's face, her hair glossy as a raven's wing in the sun.

Amanda shifted in the saddle, unwilling to watch Cathrene cast her considerable charm on Reid. "I'll walk the roan around in the yard while we're waiting." She lifted the reins and was about to move away when a small figure came out of the house and skipped down the steps. "Amanda!" Janie called. "Are you going riding?"

The stallion neighed and bobbed its head nervously at the sound of Janie's high-pitched voice. Reid turned and Janie danced down the sidewalk to run across the yard to him. Just then, the stallion gave its final tug and was free. The horse turned to make a mad dash for freedom and found Janie staring up at him, her eyes round with fright.

"No, Karma," she cried, and reached for the reins that dangled from the horse's bridle.

"Janie, no," Amanda cried. "Let him go."

Wrapping the reins around her small hand as she had been taught to do when she wanted to keep a horse from running away, she shook her head and began to walk back toward the hitching rail, leading the horse. The stallion seemed too stunned to resist. Janie had almost reached the rail when Amanda saw the muscles bunching in the stallion's powerful rear end and the hind legs tensing to rear. His ears were pulled back flat against his head.

Amanda leaned over the neck of the roan and took it in at the stallion on a dead run. The stallion heard the other horse coming. Surprised and thrown off balance, the stallion turned to protect its flank from this new and unwanted threat. Amanda half fell, half jumped off the horse, dimly aware that Reid was shouting. She scrambled to her feet, her hands tearing frantically at Janie's. The stallion turned on the roan, neighing, and reared, dragging Janie off her feet and Amanda with her, tumbling both girls on the ground. Janie was tangled in the reins more firmly than ever. One was wrapped around her waist, and she held the other in a death grip that Amanda couldn't loosen. "Let go, Janie," she cried through gritted teeth, but the young girl's eyes were glazed with terror. Amanda was sure she hadn't heard her at all. Dust was acrid in Amanda's nose along with the smell of hot, excited horseflesh and their sweating fear. A prolonged female scream seemed to go on and on over the neighing of the horses.

"Dammit, get that roan out of here," she heard Reid order someone. "My God, Amanda, *get away from that horse!*" Hard hands reached for her, but she eluded them. She held on to Janie with a death grip of her own, tugging frantically at the leather straps, which might have been iron chains. She felt the stallion's hot breath against her skin, but at last, miraculously, Janie was free and on her feet. Amanda gave her a desperate push away from danger and saw one of the ranch hands reach for Janie and gather her into his arms. Her body sagging with relief, Amanda took a step away from the melee. She felt the hard grasp of Reid's hands on her upper arms and looked up into his face. It was contorted with pain.

"Amanda!" It was a frantic, primitive cry followed by searing pain, hot and metallic, slashing down the side of her head. She heard Reid's choked cry and his heated cursing, and then the earth turned and whirled and receded suddenly into blessed blackness.

* * *

150

Her whole head throbbed with pain. She tried to open her eyes but they were heavy and uncooperative. She was in a bed in her nightgown, that much she knew. She lifted her eyelids. The room she was in was dimly lit from a lamp somewhere behind her head. Pale turquoise drapes at the windows told her she was in Reid's room. Then she saw him. He was standing with his back to her, looking out of the window into the darkness. Something about him, the way he held his shoulders, the lift of his head disturbed her. He might have been as distant as the moon.

"Reid." Her voice was husky, her throat dry, but the sound of his name was comforting. Yet he didn't turn. "What . . . what time is it?"

He turned and gazed down at her, a light flaring in his eyes. It disappeared and his eyelids flickered down. She had hoped he would take her in his arms and comfort her. He was dressed formally in a cream-colored suit of fine wool and a matching shirt, his tie dark and formally correct. Like his manner. He made no move to come near her. "A little after eight in the evening."

"What . . . what happened?" She stared at him, knowing something was dreadfully wrong.

"The stallion caught you with one of its hooves," he said. "You've been unconscious for most of the day. The doctor has bandaged the gash on your head and pronounced you all right otherwise. No broken bones or permanent damage. You were . . . lucky." He gazed at her with darkly hooded eyes. "The doctor has recommended that you stay in bed tomorrow in case you experience some dizziness from your head wound." His mouth twisted. "I felt it was my duty to notify your father that you would be staying here a few more days." He turned abruptly to look out the window again. "It was a mistake," he said coolly. "He became overwrought. He blamed me for your becoming injured. When I assured him that I . . . was as concerned for your welfare as he was because I had asked you to be my wife, his agitation increased. He blamed himself for . . . endangering you. He wants you to forget everything . . . and come home."

He turned around and came toward her then. But when he sat down on the bed, propping himself up with a hand on either side of her, his manner was faintly menacing, far from that of the ardent lover he had been the night before. "What did he mean, Amanda?"

She closed her eyes and turned her head. It throbbed painfully. She raised a hand to her brow, shielding her face from his ice-cool eyes. "It . . . it isn't important."

"Damn you!" His voice was low and fury-laden. Uncaring of her wound, he grasped her hand and dragged it away from her head. "You came here to plead your father's case with me, didn't you?"

"Is . . . is that so wrong?" she asked softly, her eyes eloquent.

His mouth lifted sardonically. "There's a name for it."

"I wasn't going to go to bed with you to earn your favor for my father."

"Weren't you? After last night, I find that hard to believe."

"That was something different, something just for us—"

His harsh crack of laughter sent a white-hot surge of anger through her. That he should immediately suspect her of using her body to bargain with him proved he had no faith in her, and no love for her at all.

"I didn't come here to seduce you," she said, furious.

"No?" His smile was not a sign of amusement. "You

152

had a damn good go at it last night, didn't you? But then I was fool enough to believe all that sweet, innocent passion and propose to you. That must have been gratifying!"

"Oh, what does it matter what I say," she cried, angry tears filling her eyes. "You won't believe me no matter how much I deny it."

"Right," he said shortly. "At least you're intelligent enough to know that."

The brush of his jacket against her arm was provocative. She wanted to cry bitterly for the loss of the world she had glimpsed in his arms. He must never know how much she needed him, how cruelly she would miss him. Just the sight of him, the press of his hip against her body, was exquisite torture.

"You're leaving," she said huskily, lifting her eyes to him. "Please, just go. I know you won't want to see me again. I . . . I'll find a way back to San Francisco. Just . . . just don't take your anger out on Susan. She knew nothing about my father or . . . or my reasons for coming."

His mouth curled in a taunting smile. "What makes you think I won't want to see you again?"

His hand, which had been lying on hers where he had thrust it over her head, slid down her bare arm and over her shoulder to circle her throat as if he were going to strangle her.

She stared up at him, unmoving, her only sign of stress a slight widening of her dark pupils.

"You're a scheming, calculating female under that cool face," he said, watching her as his restraining hand became a caressing one. "But you respond to my touch like a wild bird." His fingers found the throbbing pulse she couldn't control. "Fighting it and loving it." His fingers began a leisurely path down the curve of her throat. She

153

lay utterly still, fighting the leap of her senses. His eyes were cool and mocking as he trailed the questing finger lower toward the top of one rounded breast. His hand paused as he assessed her reaction. Emerald eyes flashed defiance at him, daring him to continue. His gray eyes glittered, and she was grasped roughly and hauled into his arms.

She braced herself for the cruelty of his mouth and was totally unprepared for his tender possessiveness. Warm and male and sensitive, the touch of his lips devastated her. She raised her hands to push him away, but he held her close and deepened the kiss, probing her mouth with his tongue, tasting her, making her aware of a deep molten core of feminine need inside her that only Reid's complete possession would ease. Hands meant to thrust him away spread over his jacket and gloried in the hard strength of his male body.

When he lifted his mouth, a soft, protesting moan escaped her. He murmured her name and his lean fingers captured her chin and throat. She didn't need his physical grasp to tell her that she was his prisoner. She was caught in his sensual spell, a captivity she wanted never to end. Yet she wanted more; she ached for the completeness of his total possession once again. When his hand brushed aside her nightgown, found the top of her breast and traced the rosy bareness of its peak, the taut response of her body brought only a heady sense of rightness.

"You're an unprincipled little witch," he murmured against her cheek. "But nothing has changed. I still want you."

His words shattered the sensual haze. "No," she whispered, remembering that he didn't love her. "Not like this. Not without love." He bent his head and kissed the top of her breast lightly. A small gasp of pleasure escaped her. From deep in his throat, he murmured huskily against her skin, "We don't need love for this."

Her heart cried out in pain. "I won't stay," she whispered fiercely. "I'll be gone when you return."

He lifted his head and gazed at her. The cynical lift of his mouth told her what he saw, feminine lips swollen with his kisses, creamy skin fiery with response to his sensual touch—a woman he had already taken to his bed. "Will you? I don't think so." His finger traced the soft area of her throat where the vein still pulsed at an accelerated rhythm. "Because if you leave tomorrow—" He paused and then said, "Your father will declare bankruptcy in a month."

"No," she whispered. "You wouldn't."

He lifted an eyebrow. "I wouldn't have to do a thing. It's already in the cards. He couldn't have handled the museum renovation. Most of the committee knew that from the beginning. And without that contract"—he shrugged, his shoulders moving under the expensive jacket—"his business will finally collapse under the weight of his debts."

A chilling picture of her father's bleak face flashed into her mind. He would be a desperate man, driven to . . . what? She didn't dare to think. She shivered and pulled the blanket up around her shoulders, thinking at that moment she must hate Reid Buchanan as much as it was humanly possible to hate another being. "I don't believe you. You're deliberately trying to frighten me. He'll get other offers. He has to."

His eyes were hooded, and she couldn't see his expression, but there was no mistaking the soft intentness of his voice. "No."

Her eyes blazed up at him. "Because you'll see to it that he doesn't," she cried. "Oh, how could I have forgotten what a despicable, self-serving man you are!"

"On the other hand," he went on casually, as if she had said nothing, "your father could begin to receive small offers in about a month, an offer, say, to remodel a house in Sausalito, or a contract to build a small housing complex in Oakland. Things he could handle easily, things he used to specialize in." He paused, watching her. "He might get three or four offers at once and even have to turn a few down." His eyes were faintly insolent. "The choice is yours."

"My God!" she cried. "You call me unprincipled. You're . . . unconscionable!"

"Am I?" He lifted an eyebrow and smiled grimly. "All I've done is play your little game, clarifying the rules and raising the stakes."

"You write your own rules," she said huskily.

"The question remains: Are you going to play the game?"

She turned her head away. "You know I can't stand by and see my father destroyed."

"Yes," he said softly. "I counted on that."

She turned back to him, her eyes brilliant. "You've won. Now, please go."

"I'm not quite finished," he said calmly. "No one must know about our little game. Everyone must believe that ours is a case of irresistible love at first sight."

She made a choked sound in her throat. "I don't understand why you care—"

"Especially Jane," he added softly. "Shall I go on?"

She made a gesture with her hand.

"I'll be in London a week. If you should need me, I can

156

be reached at this number." He plucked a white card from his inside jacket pocket and laid it on the night stand. "When I return, we'll fly to New York . . . together."

He rose and looked down at her. "One other thing, Amanda. There'll be no outside amusements." His lean face tightened. "Forget about Colin."

Anger flashed from her eyes. "Does that restriction apply just to me, or does it include you, too?"

His eyes glittered down at her through a long, still silence. "Would it bother you if I took a lover?"

Challenged, she retreated. "You . . . you said our marriage was supposed to look like a love match. If you take other women to bed, it certainly won't."

The corners of his mouth turned up in the first sign of amusement she had seen that evening. "I'm a normal man with normal male appetites." His eyes traveled slowly over the outline of her body under the light coverlet. "If you don't want other women in my bed, you'd better be there yourself."

Her expression of rage made him laugh softly. "Goodbye, darling. I'll see you in a week. Try to contain your impatience."

She heard the soft click of the light. The room was plunged into darkness. He was gone. She was left to wrestle with her hatred and her anger, her utter desolation . . . and her longing for him.

She didn't sleep well that night. When Susan came in the next morning, Amanda was grateful the kick of the stallion could be blamed for the state of her eyes.

Susan sat down next to her, her eyes alight with curiosity and excitement. "I can't believe it," she said directly. "You and Reid. You never said a word."

Amanda felt chilled. "He's told everyone, then."

"Of course," Susan said and laughed. "You didn't expect him to keep it a secret, did you? He's too proud of himself for that." Susan dropped her hand to Amanda's on the coverlet. "He's crazy about you. Everyone was really surprised, except Jane."

"How . . . how did she take the news?" Amanda asked anxiously.

Susan tilted her head to one side. "Quietly. As if she knew it all along. Did she?"

Amanda said softly, "No. She couldn't have."

"Isn't it exciting? You've known each other such a short time. Aren't you thrilled, Amanda? Everyone thought Reid would never marry. Now he is, and to you. We can have a double wedding—"

"No!" Amanda cried out, and then more softly, "no. I . . . I don't want to take away from your day, darling. Please—"

Susan's eyes clouded. "But it's already been discussed. I suggested it to David, and he talked to Reid about it. He had no objections." She looked down at Amanda. "Is something wrong? You . . . you do love him, don't you?"

Amanda smiled faintly. "Of course, darling." She added with an ironic tone that Susan missed, "You of all people should know how irresistible the Buchanan men are."

Susan smiled. "Oh, I know, all right. I just never thought you were susceptible after Colin."

Amanda's smile was rueful. "That was what made Reid all the more dangerous. I thought I was immune." She glanced at Susan's neat suit, her sandaled feet. "Are you leaving this morning?"

Her sister nodded. "Reid organized it. Since he had to leave for London earlier than he had planned, he hired a pilot from Olancha to take us back. He suggested I go back and hold Dad's hand. Reid said he was frantic on the phone about you."

Amanda grasped Susan's wrist. "Please, tell Dad I'm fine. I'll be home in a few days and . . . I'll talk to him then."

"Don't worry about him, Amanda." Susan rose. "I suppose I better go. David and the pilot are waiting for me. I'll soothe Dad. I suppose it will be a shock to him, losing us both at the same time, but it can't be helped."

"No," Amanda murmured, "it can't be helped."

She tried to keep that in mind as she climbed out of bed and padded to the closet. There was about one's life an inevitability, a fate. She had been fated to be Reid's from the day she had stood in his arms on Fisherman's Wharf and felt her soul claimed.

She opened the closet and saw among her other things a blouse of pale green silk, classically cut, with a pointed collar and long sleeves with buttoned cuffs. She thought of Cathrene's flair for wearing silk with rougher fabrics and slipped into it, tucking it into the waistband of her khaki pants. She arranged her hair around the bandage on the back of her head as best she could, letting it lie loosely around her shoulders. She looked into the mirror and shuddered. A purple bruise lay on her left cheekbone, and her eyes were dark and sunken. She hardly looked like the fiancée of a wealthy and influential man, a woman radiant with love.

But she would have to put on a facade. Resolutely, she squared her shoulders and opened the door to stare directly into the eyes of a gray-haired woman as startled as she was, attempting to balance a tray in her hands.

"Oh, I'm sorry," Amanda said. "Can I help you?"

"Your sister said you were awake. I was just bringing you your breakfast. The doctor did say you were to stay in bed today, you know."

"I'm not ill." Amanda looked down at the tray, attractively arranged with orange juice, toast, and coffee on white china. On one side lay a single white rose. "It's lovely," she said, glancing back into the woman's eyes. "You're Tessa, aren't you?"

The woman nodded. "Everyone's outside. Would you like to come in the kitchen and keep me company while you eat? I've just started a batch of strawberry jam." The woman's step was brisk as she led the way back to the kitchen. She set the food on the butcher-block table that stood in a circular window bay. She brought a crystal bud vase out from a cabinet and put the rose in it.

"Thank you," Amanda said huskily, deeply touched by the woman's warm, caring gesture. She slid into the curved leather seat that surrounded the table and unfolded the linen napkin.

"Thank *you*," Tessa said, looking down at her. "It's a small token of our thanks for saving our daughter. The rose is from our garden."

Amanda tried to shake her head, but winced from the pain. "I'm not sure I really did that much."

"Aren't you?" Tessa shook her head. "Have you looked in the mirror this morning?"

Amanda smiled. "I have, unfortunately."

"Then how do you think Janie would have looked this morning if you hadn't come to her rescue? She might even be—"

Amanda shook her head. "I don't think so."

"Well." The woman turned and with a determined air began stemming strawberries from a box piled high with

160

red fruit. "Nevertheless, John and I want you to know we're very grateful. That's the kind of thing you can never really repay." She glanced around at Amanda. "You'll discover that for yourself when you're a mother. Having children is . . . it makes you terribly vulnerable. You want to protect them, give them everything. You would move the earth for them if you could." Tessa sighed. "We're terribly doting parents, I'm afraid. We'd been married so long. We'd almost given up hope of having children. Then, a miracle! Tim was born and in a few more years Janie came along. We were ecstatic."

Amanda sipped her coffee, gaining some comfort from the hot liquid.

"Jane said you were ill. I hope your husband is better today, too," Amanda said, hoping to stop the woman's deluge of gratitude and her testimony to the joy of parenthood. It made the weight against Amanda's heart seem even heavier.

"He's down at the branding pens," she said. "He would get up today. No holding him back." Her voice betrayed her fond pride. "He thinks this ranch can't do without him." Deftly, she tossed several berries into the bowl. "But I suspect it could. Tim handled the roundup well enough."

"You're very fortunate, Tessa." The toast felt dry in her mouth. "You have a family to be proud of."

"We're so pleased that you're going to be a part of it," she went on, her choice of topic even less desirable to Amanda. "Janie's absolutely thrilled. She took to you so quick."

"I like Janie very much. I . . . do you think anyone would mind if I walked down to watch the branding?"

"No, of course not," Tessa assured her warmly. Then

with a little anxious frown touching her brows, she said, "Are you sure you feel well enough? You didn't do anymore than peck at that breakfast."

"I'm fine," Amanda said firmly. "I've never fainted in my life."

"I don't know," the older woman said, shaking her head. "If Reid found out I went against his orders and let you up out of bed, he'd probably have my hide and hang it on the wall. He told me you were to stay in bed and rest."

"Well, what he doesn't know won't hurt him, will it?" Amanda said lightly.

Tessa eyed her with a shrewd glance. "No, I guess not, except if you know Reid at all, you know there isn't much that misses him. He was always a smart little devil. I could never outguess him as a child. Seems like he hasn't changed much, either. He sure surprised everyone with your engagement." She turned to gaze over Amanda's shoulder out toward the mountains. Amanda had no choice but to sit quietly and listen. "I used to worry about him. I knew this ranch wasn't big enough to contain that restless energy of his. He'd go off for hours at a time to be alone. Then he'd race into the yard, saddle up a horse, and ride like the devil down the road. Yet he was tied to the land somehow, too. I sometimes think he has to come back every so often just to get the smell of cattle in his nose." She shook her head. "He wasn't an easy child to know. He was quiet. You never knew what he was thinking. Now, David, he was made of different stuff. You always knew where you stood with David. He liked to talk, and he was easygoing and uncomplicated." Tessa shook her head again. "That's the way kids are, I guess, different. My Tim is quiet, but he's happy. Janie, she's another story. She's quiet, but like Reid was. Reads a lot, too."

"She's a very intense little girl," Amanda said thoughtfully, telling herself she was glad the conversation had turned away from Reid, yet strangely moved by Tessa's portrait of the young Reid.

With a quick glance upward at the bold, modern face of the clock that hung on the wall, Tessa moved to the sink. "Those men will be working up a thirst. I'd better get this lemonade down to them."

"I'll take it," Amanda offered quickly.

"Are you sure?" Tessa asked.

Amanda answered by lifting the green jug out of Tessa's hands. "Don't forget the paper cups," Tessa said, smilingly offering her a large brown-paper bag to tuck under her other arm. The tantalizing smell of cooking strawberries drifted to Amanda's nose from the bubbling pot on the stove. Tessa smiled.

"There's homemade bread and strawberry jam for lunch," she said. "Maybe you'll have more appetite after you've been outside."

"Maybe I will," Amanda said, and turned to go, smiling.

CHAPTER 8

Calves whined, cattle bawled. Amanda walked over the dusty earth toward the branding corral, the jug swinging at her side, the heels of her riding boots digging into the soft earth. The air was full of dust and sound. She reached the rail fence and rested the jug on top of it. Men in blue denim and red cattle milled in the pen together. One cowboy on the back of a black horse separated a calf from the rest of the herd. The calf's white face twisted in pain as its hind legs collapsed from the loop of the rope and its front legs were quickly secured by another rope. A branding iron was held against the rear flank of the protesting calf. Amanda wrinkled her nose at the smell of the burning flesh and hair. Another cowboy dabbed the wound with a smelly disinfectant. Something was done to the calf's ears and then the ropes were stripped off. The calf scrambled to its feet and ran into the protection of the rest of the herd, finding its mother quickly.

There was a movement beside her. She turned to see Bob Conroy standing at her side, watching the action with an amused smile. He turned to her. "Feeling sorry for them?" He nodded toward the next calf that had already fallen under the cowboy's rope and the horse's practiced bracing of feet.

"Yes, a little," Amanda said.

"Don't," he bit out. "That's steak on your table."

"I guess I'd rather not think of that right now," Amanda said honestly. "Why is that one being branded twice?"

"It's a heifer," he said softly. "It's been chosen for breeding." He turned sharp blue eyes to her. "Something like you."

"Stop it!" she said sharply, a spot of red appearing on each cheek, giving her bruise a more vivid color.

"It's the truth, isn't it? You were brought out here for Jane's approval. You won that hands down."

"It wasn't like that at all." She gazed out over the cattle. "Why do the heifers have to wear two brands?"

He smiled at her determined effort to keep the conversation impersonal. "Only the cattle kept at the ranch are marked with the Circle B brand. The others, the ones that are going to be sold, get the number thirty-four on their flank. That's Jane's number. It identifies any stock wearing that number as hers. Careful records are kept of any cattle sold wearing that brand."

"Does that stop people from stealing cattle?"

Bob Conroy shrugged. "Nothing stops some people. But it's a deterrent."

The man on the black horse caught sight of them and waved his hat. He rode to them and dismounted on the other side of the fence. Tall and stocky, his face wore the lines of many summers and winters spent looking for cattle on the range. His graying hair was cut short and his mouth was turned up in a smile. "I'm John Montgomery," he said, thrusting his hand over the fence at her. "I want to say thank you for what you did for my daughter."

She took his hard, calloused hand. "It was nothing."

The jug and the paper bag of cups were passed over the fence to him.

"That's a matter of opinion," he said, his hazel eyes twinkling. "I've hated that stallion ever since Josh bought him. I guess I won't have to hate him anymore now."

"Why not?" Amanda asked.

John Montgomery shot a quick glance at Bob Conroy. "I thought she knew," he said in a low tone. Then, looking back at Amanda, he said, "Reid ordered the animal shot." At Amanda's indrawn breath, he said quickly, "Believe me, no one was sorry. Even Josh thought it should be done. It hadn't been broken properly when he bought it. He only kept it because Cathrene liked it. She's a gal who likes to live dangerously."

Amanda felt shaken. "But to shoot a beautiful horse like that just because—"

"I'll breathe easier about Janie," John Montgomery said, saying the one thing that would make Amanda regret the horse's death much less. "Well, thanks for the lemonade." He walked purposefully away, taking the jug to a tree in the yard. Soon the men were standing around him, lifting cups to their mouths.

"Were you planning on riding this morning?"

"I don't know," Amanda said coolly. "Why?"

Bob Conroy's mouth tightened. "Because I'd like to get some sleep if you aren't," he said wearily. "I've been up all night. But my orders are to ride with you mornings if that's what you want. It doesn't make any difference to me what you do. I'm just trying to figure out when I'm going to get some sleep."

Amanda raised her head and stared at him. "I don't need you watchdogging me. I'm perfectly capable of riding by myself and taking care of myself."

"You're about as capable as a two-day-old colt," he said scathingly.

"Who's going to bother me out here? Really, I—"

"We have a steady stream of backpackers and campers up and down that road." He pointed to the highway. "The Sierras attract city people by the dozens. So if you think you're safe just because you're out of the city, forget it. Now, are you going riding or not?"

She shook her head. "No." She turned to walk away from him.

He caught her wrist and turned her around. "Don't even think of it."

"I don't know what you're talking about," she said, shaking her arm to free it from his grasp.

He didn't let go. "Don't think of saddling the horse and going out on your own. That's one thing Buchanan and I agree on. You're *not* to ride alone."

She stared at him, her face cool.

"Look," he said, dropping her wrist. "You don't look as if you belong on the back of a horse at all today. How about planning something for tomorrow?"

"What time?" She hated herself for giving in, but she wanted desperately to ride.

"Tom comes on duty at six. So any time after that."

"Six oh five," Amanda said coolly. "That way, you can get your duty ride out of the way and get to bed immediately afterwards."

He made an exasperated sound. "Look, Miss Kirk— Amanda! You know I don't feel that way."

She stared at him, her eyes frosty, not knowing whether that was worse or better. "I'll see you tomorrow morning, Mr. Conroy."

167

He released her arm, his shrug almost Gallic. "Fine. I'll see you then."

She hadn't meant to enjoy riding with him. She couldn't help herself. Every morning for three days they went out, galloping along the track toward the rising sun, a sun that pierced the mountain peaks and spread fingers of light through their jagged edges, pouring pale gold over earth and sky. The air was crisp and clean and she was thankful for the wool-lined jacket Tessa had loaned her.

They began to talk, carefully at first, discussing the kinds of pine trees that grew in the Sierras, the history of the mountains, the difficulty of climbing Half Dome, and the indomitable spirit of John Muir, who walked the Sierras and wrote of their beauty.

On the third morning, they rode to the foothills and reined in beside a small stream. A clearing surrounded by pines stood to their left, and the horses rested there, snorting and blowing softly. The tightly curled buds of California poppy lay at Amanda's feet. They had not yet opened their faces to the sun. She found a smooth stone and sat down, lifting her own features to the warmth of the sun's rays.

"I love this so much it seems almost sinful," she said. Bob stretched out on the ground beside her and pulled his Stetson down over his eyes. "You're tired," she said, "and we've come farther than we usually do."

"Sit still," he said, the hat muffling his words.

"I'll soon be gone," she said lightly. "Then you'll be able to sleep as much as you want."

"Be quiet," he said, his voice low.

She stared out over the flatlands and saw the stand of cottonwoods that surrounded the ranch house. Bob tilted the hat from his face, laying it against the back of his head. "What are you thinking about?" he asked.

"I was wondering about you," she said lightly. "Are you going to spend the rest of your life here in Owens Valley as a ranch hand?"

"What if I were?"

She moved her shoulders. "I . . . I think you're too intelligent to be working for somebody else all the time."

"As a matter of fact, I am leaving at the end of the season."

"Where will you go?"

He shrugged. "Hawaii, Alaska, Australia. Who knows?"

"You don't ever plan to settle down, have a family?" He stacked one booted foot up on the toe of the other, his legs long and lean in the blue denim. His eyes were dark, half hidden under his hat. "I'm not as family-oriented as some people are."

"Where are your parents?"

"Dead," he said bluntly. "Dad had a ranch in Colorado. He and Mom were killed in an automobile accident when I was a child. Dad's brother took over the ranch. He didn't care for me much. I stayed till I couldn't stand it anymore. Then I got out. But all I knew was ranching. So I ended up here."

"How old were you when you left your uncle's ranch?"

"Fourteen," he said, gazing up at the sky.

"Fourteen? You were still a boy."

"I could do a man's work," he said flatly. He shifted his body and sat up to look at her. His eyes traveled over her face. All signs of the bruising were gone. The days of good food and exercise had brought a sparkle to her eyes, a healthy glow to her skin. She wore jeans and a blouse, but she was alive, almost shimmering with life, and incredibly attractive to him.

"What about you? Seems to me you're going to make a damn poor executive's wife."

"Thanks," she said shortly.

"That's not what I meant," he said. "If this is what you enjoy"—he swept a hand around at the mountains and trees and then nodded at the horses—"you're not going to fit into the social whirl Buchanan maintains."

"I'll have to, won't I?"

"Knowing you, you probably will." He squinted skyward. "See that hawk?"

She tilted her head, spotting the drifting bird as it rode on an air current above them.

"Take it away from these mountains and it will die."

"That isn't surprising."

"It needs the mountain air to breathe."

"I suppose so—" She frowned, not knowing exactly what he was getting at.

"People need to be loved, just like that hawk needs to breathe in mountain air," he said huskily, startling her.

"That's true," she said, her own voice lowering, feeling touched by the seriousness of his words and remembering how desolate she had felt when she had finally realized Colin didn't love her. "How . . . how did you know?"

"How do I know?" he grated. "Because I had love once and it was taken away from me."

"You must have loved your parents very much."

He leaned forward, grasping her hand, his fingers warm. "I'd give anything to feel that total, complete, *tolerant* love again." His eyes burned at her. "Don't do it, Amanda. Don't sell yourself to Buchanan. It isn't worth it."

170

"I . . . I don't know what you're talking about." For one startled moment she thought he must know the truth about her and her father, about everything.

"Buchanan's rich, sure. But he can't give you his love. He doesn't have any to give. He's lived in a dog-eat-dog world for so long he's forgotten people like you exist."

"Bob, don't put me up on a pedestal. I . . . I don't belong there."

"Maybe not." His eyes held hers. "But you're real and honest, the kind of woman that needs to be loved."

"No, no. Sometimes I'm not that, either."

"Amanda, I—" He drew her closer.

"No, don't," she said, feeling a strange repugnance, a guilt. "Don't say any more." She got to her feet, pulling her hand from his grasp.

He stood staring at her for a long moment, then picked his hat up off the ground and hit it against his legs. "Sure," he said curtly.

"Bob, please, I appreciate what you've done for me," she said, and it was true. He had filled the vacuum of her mind—and taken away the sting of knowing Reid had no intention of calling her.

Bob's mouth twisted. "Don't brush me off with a few polite phrases as if I were a toy Buchanan left you to amuse yourself with! I was wrong about you, wasn't I?" He gazed at her, his eyes contemptuous. "You can be bought. You have been."

A bird sang somewhere in the mountains. It was a poignant, lilting melody. She stared into Bob Conroy's taut face, longing to deny his words, knowing she couldn't.

"We'd better go back," he said roughly. "I'll get the horses."

She remembered the look in his eyes as she wandered that afternoon in the apple orchard. She walked slowly from tree to tree, touching the rough bark, rubbing the leaves between her fingers. Was she trying to touch reality? She didn't know. Her father had called last night and he had seemed calmer. She had almost convinced him she was marrying Buchanan because she loved him. But it was far too late. The damage had been done.

She shuddered. This endless waiting for Reid to return was getting on her nerves. She thought he would come back yesterday. There had been no word from him. She hadn't expected any. At night, she endured his ghost, the ghost that haunted her with words of love.

You need love, her mind cried that night, echoing Bob Conroy's words. *You need love,* the cottonwood leaves seemed to rustle and whisper in reply. But whatever she needed, it was all wrapped up in the lean male body of Reid Buchanan. He filled all her thoughts, waking and sleeping. He had driven out thoughts of Colin in one day and caressed her to a fevered pitch of desire in one night. Whatever he was, whatever he had to give her, it was all she would ever have. She needed him like a thirsty man in the desert needs that first sip of water in order to live again.

A knock sounded at her door in the early-morning darkness. She rolled over and lifted her watch from the night stand. The red numbers read five thirty. "Go away, Bob," she groaned softly.

The soft, faint creak of the door opening shocked her into complete wakefulness. Her eyes flew open and her fingers grasped at the covers, pulling them over her slightly clad body.

"Were you expecting him?" It was Reid's soft, husky

172

tone, not Bob's, that met her ears. Strangely enough, she relaxed. Then she heard the sound of the door closing and Reid's booted foot on the floor, and her tension returned in double strength. For Reid's hard, lean body dressed in a suede wool-lined jacket and denim shirt and jeans was dipping the mattress next to her. She longed to close her eyes and feign sleep, but his gray ones were already laughing down at her.

The laughter faded and desire burned there, a desire she could see and feel. She was powerless to move. He picked up a strand of fiery hair that lay spilled out over the pillow. "So this is what you look like in the morning, all warm and sleepy." He bent to touch his lips lightly to the strand he held. "You smell like lilacs," he murmured, breathing in the scent of her skin. She fought the urge to slip her arms around his neck, pull his head down, slide his mouth to hers, and kiss him deeply. His hair still curled damply around his ears and neck from his shower. It tantalized her. He smelled so male and clean, his jacket and lining rough and crisp against her skin where the nightgown left her throat bare, that it struck her how extremely pleasant it would be to wake in the arms of this man every morning. He sat up, a slight smile lifting his lips as if he could read her thoughts. "You haven't said good morning to me, Amanda. Has the cat got that lovely tongue of yours?"

"I . . . I didn't know you were back," she said huskily.

He reached out to her, as if compelled to touch her. His tracing finger brushed one red-gold eyebrow and then wandered lower to stroke the rise of her cheekbone. "Are you disappointed?"

"No," she said honestly, a faint blush coloring her skin.

"Did you miss me a little?"

She lay still, trying to ignore the tingling response at the

173

base of her spine to those feather-light fingers on her face. "I'm glad you're back safely," she hedged, her breath quickening.

He laughed softly. "You're a liar and a fraud, Amanda Kirk." His voice teased rather than accused. "I knew it from the moment I saw you. There's passion under that cool smile, so much passion you're terrified of what you might feel if you let yourself go."

He bent swiftly and took her lips. She struggled, trying to push him away. He would not be moved. He warmed her lips with his and then probed her mouth with his tongue until all thought of resistance vanished.

He drew the covers away and dispensed with the fragile barrier of her nightgown. In the soft light of the room, she lay naked before him and unashamed. It was so right and natural that Reid should be the man to admire her womanly curves.

And he *was* admiring them. His eyes gleamed over her for a long, silent moment. Then he groaned softly and lifted her into his arms. His face deep in the soft silk of her hair, he murmured, "My God, you're beautiful and so unaware."

He kissed her mouth and then let her lie back down on the bed. He bent his head and his thick black hair brushed her skin as his mouth claimed a taut nipple. His hand made forays of its own, in a smooth caress over her abdomen, feathering across her hipbone and down to the inner curve of her thigh. Desire seared through her, every inch of her body flooded with a white-hot hunger. Drugged by the warm, male scent of him and the wild need burning inside her, she whispered, "Reid, I—"

He lifted his head, a smile touching his mouth. She clung to him and arched her breasts against the rough fabric of his shirt, her body telling him of her need more eloquently than any words could. His voice was soft. "I know, darling, I know." And then he put her gently away.

Shattered by his rejection, she pulled the covers over her naked body and turned her face into the pillow. He took her chin in his hand, forcing her to look at him. "Amanda, don't."

"Don't what?" she murmured. She lay silent, her eyes fastened on the lining of his jacket.

His soft laugh was a low, pleasant sound. "Don't think you've fooled me for a minute. But I'm not going to start our life together with you calling the tune, darling." He leaned forward and kissed her lightly and then stood up. "I almost came to kiss you awake directly from my shower," he said, his voice low and intense. "It's a good thing I didn't." He looked down at her, his eyes moving over the outline of her curves not quite hidden by the bedcovers. "You'd better get up and get dressed before my control deserts me. I'll meet you outside in five minutes," he said, his voice husky. "And be quick. Because if you aren't"—there was an amused glitter in his eyes—"I might change my mind about accepting your invitation and join you in bed." He went out, laughing softly. She tried to be angry. But she couldn't.

She showered, dressed quickly, and slipped into Tessa's jacket. She couldn't deny that she was looking forward to riding with Reid. She couldn't deny that walking into the cool morning air and seeing him standing casually, his suede coat open, holding the reins of the roan and his palomino, gave her a pang of pleasure that was sensual, a sexual excitement. Reid was a male animal in superb condition, lean and attractive. He wore no hat and the breeze lifted his glossy dark hair away from his forehead.

175

"Seven minutes," he said, handing her the reins to the roan. "In another two I'd have gone back to your room." She put a foot into the stirrup. A lean hand curved itself against her bottom, boosting her up onto the horse, giving her a shock that ran through every nerve. She colored. He swung up into the saddle, laughing. "But then we wouldn't have gone for our ride," he said, smiling at her from the horse's back. "Or anywhere else for the rest of the day."

Her face crimson, she lifted the reins and whirled the roan away from the palomino to set the pace with a fast and furious gallop.

She looked at the passenger seated next to her in the jet plane that afternoon and wondered if this formally dressed male could possibly be the same man who only this morning had teased her unmercifully and then talked with her seriously, telling her of his love for the land, his hope to keep the ranch in his family always, his belief that man was merely a steward of the land, that God lent man the earth briefly and expected man to tend it carefully. If a woman was thought to possess a dozen different faces, a dozen different personalities, surely a man did, too. She could hardly equate that earthy man with this executive in the light gray suit of fine wool that fit like a tailor's dream over the lean male body. They might have been two different men. Before they had been in the air an hour, he had dealt with three major crises by phone: something that had to do with that same cost sheet in a Nevada copper mine he had been calling about the other night, a labor dispute at a television station in Florida, and some snag in offshore oil prospecting in the Gulf of Mexico.

She put her head back against the seat and watched him

from behind lowered lids, seeing him in a business setting for the first time since that disastrous day he had badgered her father so unmercifully. In the space of two weeks he had proposed to her and refused to let her go. For the first time, she wondered why he had insisted on marriage. He didn't love her. Anxiety stirred. Did he have some ulterior motive for wanting to marry her? He had made a devil's bargain with her and then carried out their engagement as if it were a normal one in every way. He had introduced her to his pilot as his fiancée. Now, in the middle of reading some papers clipped together, he glanced up at her. "Bored, darling?" The endearment came easily to his lips.

She shook her head. "Just wondering what Milton will say."

Reid returned his attention to his reading material. "Hard to tell," he murmured. "It won't make a difference, anyway."

And with that one sentence he dismissed Milton's reactions.

New York looked much the same, although it was summer now. The air conditioning hummed in Milton's office as they entered. The modern paintings of ballet dancers and a collage of singers still hung on the cream walls, and the dark blue carpeting still looked as if it needed vacuuming. Yet there were changes. Her desk had been angled away from Milton's door and an ivy in an intricate macramé hanger of jute hung in front of the tall window. And the girl who sat at her typewriter was slim and blond.

"May I help you—" Her smile flashed directly at Reid. "Oh, hello, Mr. Buchanan."

"Hello, Judy," he said amicably, astounding Amanda

by calling the girl by her given name. "How are things going?"

"Super," the girl said, her eyes shining. "I love it here. I really appreciate your finding me this job." The girl's bright blue eyes moved over Amanda's neat blue suit, her coppery hair done up at her nape. "Is this Amanda?"

Reid nodded, and Amanda watched the girl rise and move toward them. She had short feathery curls of fashionably silver-gold hair and her slender body was clad in a blue silk dress that clung to every line and matched her startling eyes. Was this yet another of the women who had known Reid's love-making? Something cold and insidious moved inside Amanda. This lovely young woman had obviously known Reid well. Very well.

The girl held out her hand to Amanda. Amanda took it, feeling more than anything else like a hypocrite. "I want to thank you for making it possible for me to get this job," the girl said irrepressibly.

Amanda felt the slim fingers in her own and said, "As it's only temporary, there's really no reason to—"

"Temporary?" The blue eyes were stricken. "You can't mean that. I've been hired permanently. I mean . . . I understood you were leaving!"

With a warning hand on Amanda's elbow, Reid said, "Amanda didn't realize the job had already been filled, Judy."

"Oh." The blonde's sigh of relief moved the lovely rounded shape of her. She released Amanda's hand. "You thought I was the temporary girl. She finished last week. I started this Monday, after Mr. Buchanan talked to Milton"—she shot a quick look at Amanda—"Mr. Wayman, I mean. It's all right, isn't it? I mean, you haven't changed your mind? You don't want your job back, do you?"

Amanda looked into the girl's anxious face, Reid's hand tight on her elbow. "No, no, I haven't changed my mind. I'm sure Milton is happy to have you here."

"I don't know about Milton," the blond girl said with another sigh of relief, her shoulders moving in a deprecatory little shrug. "But my husband is ecstatic. He was transferred here six months ago—he works for Mr. Buchanan—but I had this great job upstate before we were married, and I just couldn't give it up. We'd been commuting on weekends to be together since last Christmas." She beamed at Reid over Amanda's shoulder. "Now we don't have to do that anymore. We really appreciate what you've done for us, Mr. Buchanan."

"My pleasure, Judy," Reid said, his voice courteous and warm.

Amanda told Judy she would call Milton sometime in the future to say good-bye since he wasn't to be in for the rest of the day. What else could she do? Everything had been taken out of her hands. She walked into the busy street with its cacophony of horns honking and traffic sounds, the familiar skyscrapers leaning down over her, and thought her jealousy of a girl who had smiled at Reid and was happily married nothing short of madness.

Reid signaled a taxi. For him, of course, it slowed and stopped. He helped her into it. "You didn't have to take me there," she said huskily, supremely conscious of him settling close to her, his trousered leg against hers. "You already had everything neatly taken care of."

The slight smile on his lips made her wonder if he knew she was irritated because she had been jealous of Judy's brilliant smiles.

"I thought you'd like to see for yourself that the girl who replaced you was happy, and as personable and reli-

179

able as you are," he said with mocking emphasis. "Was I wrong?"

"You could have just told me," she said coolly. "I didn't need to see how happy she was."

"Would you have believed me if I had told you?"

She didn't answer. She looked away onto the busy city street.

"Your escape hatch is closed, Amanda," he said softly. "There'll be no running away from marriage this time."

"I don't know what you're talking about," she said. "I can't run away from you. You'll destroy my father if I do. I didn't run from Colin. He broke off our engagement."

"I've found you to be courageous, Amanda," he said, keeping his voice low. "You fling yourself at angry executives and ill-trained horses with equal speed and force if someone you love is in danger. If you had really loved Colin, if you had truly believed you were meant for him, you would have stayed in San Francisco and fought Lisa. You would have stayed and looked Colin and everybody else straight in the eye and done your best to win him back. You had every opportunity. You were an excellent secretary, and Colin would never have fired you. Even after he married Lisa, the battle wouldn't have been over. You would have been there in his office with him every day. You could have become his mistress," he said huskily, "and you would have—if you had really loved him."

Color flared in her cheeks. He took her hand and began caressing it with such gentleness she couldn't pull away. "But you didn't. You ran away from him, as far as you could possibly run." His gray eyes fastened on her. There was a strange and brilliant light burning in them. "Isn't it possible you knew he wasn't the man for you? Isn't it possible you got just a little tired of mothering him?"

"That's preposterous," she said, snatching her hand away. "I didn't mother Colin, ever!"

"Didn't you?" he persisted. "You saw him a year. In all that time, did he ever try to make love to you? Or"—more softly—"you to him, as you did with me?"

"You're wasted as an executive, you know," she said sharply. "You should have been a psychiatrist."

"You have to know people to lead them and run organizations," he said implacably. He continued to hold her hand, and she felt the strength in his fingers. Had he been right about her? Was there only one thing she was really afraid of, the honest, compelling, and totally consuming passion she felt as a woman? "I'm closing your escape hatch," he had said. She thought of those words as she walked into the dark-blue-velvet world of the expensive jeweler on Fifth Avenue and felt Reid's hand on her arm. He led her into a private room he had already reserved. There in the presence of a discreet man who proffered trays of rings like an automaton Reid's hand went unerringly to one of exquisite beauty. It wasn't a ring so much as a loop of gold that swooped up to a peak. On that peak, alone in flashing splendor, nestled the most beautifully faceted diamond she had ever seen. It took her breath away. Reid chose their wedding rings, too, wide bands of gold that he had sized to his and Amanda's fingers and then requested engraved with their names and the date of their wedding. She wondered how many women had found out the date of their marriage that way. It was to be in July, after Susan's. The man left as quietly as he had come, and Reid slipped the ring on her finger and then kissed her lightly with little emotion. They came out into the sunshine, blinking, and then made a wearying round of the shops, where Reid ordered more clothes than she thought she could wear in a lifetime. It was sheer relief to climb back on the plane and fly to San Francisco. Reid had incredible energy.

They arrived very late that evening and drove to her father's apartment through the first wisps of fog drifting in from the sea. When they got to the apartment, Maxwell Kirk opened the door to greet them wearing a robe and pajamas. He took Amanda in his arms to give her an enveloping hug, and then invited them both in, giving Reid a wary look. Amanda thought her father looked much better.

"It's so good to see you," Kirk said, his eyes flickering anxiously over Amanda, searching her face for signs of distress, and then falling to the brilliance of the ring on her hand. "How elegant you look," he said obliquely.

Amanda slipped out of the jacket she was wearing. It was pale green linen with a matching dress underneath. It had looked so stunning on her that Reid had insisted she change into it after seeing her try it on. The night had been chilly driving through the fog, but now she suddenly felt warm and restive.

"Did you have a good flight," her father asked.

"We came in through the fog, but yes, it was pleasant," Amanda said. "How are you, Father?"

"Never better," he said cheerfully, drawing Amanda to the sofa and sitting down next to her. "You wouldn't believe it, Amanda." Out of the corner of her eye, Amanda saw Reid wander to the mantel facade and rest his elbow against it, his face enigmatic. The back of his head was visible in the mirror, the fine silken hairs dark over his nape, the shape of his head aesthetically pleasing to the eye.

"Not getting that museum contract was the best thing

that could have happened. There was a doctor there at the meeting, a William Brown. Remember my introducing him to you? He has a cliff house in Sausalito"—her eyes flickered to Reid, who smiled faintly—"he wants me to renovate. It's not definite yet, but he should have a firm decision for me by the middle of next month. And I've had a call from a builder in Oakland. Seems he's over-extended himself and wants my company to help him. I've hired Benita back and—" Maxwell Kirk stopped speaking suddenly. He twisted his head around to Reid. "I suppose you find this all hard to believe."

There wasn't a glimmer of mockery in Reid Buchanan's eyes. "Not at all, Kirk." His eyes fastened on Amanda. "I would say it's time you had some good fortune come your way. For Amanda's sake"—she was sure only she heard the faint emphasis on her name—"I'm glad." Reid straightened away from the fireplace. "I'll be going, Amanda. Would you see me to the door?"

"I'll be going along to bed now that you're home safely," Maxwell Kirk said to Amanda. "I'll talk to you in the morning." He walked quickly across the room to the hallway and disappeared inside his bedroom.

Reid watched him go, a smile lifting his lips. Then he reached for her hand, the one that wore his ring. "Nice to think he trusts me with you," he murmured.

"Why shouldn't he?" Amanda said, her breath almost catching in her throat as he turned her hand and pressed his mouth against her palm. "You've made your honorable intentions very clear. Right from the first."

He wrapped her in his arms, his mouth against her temple. "I told you when we first met I didn't believe in wasting time." He kissed her forehead lightly. "You've had a long day. I have to fly out tonight to London,

183

Amanda. I'll be at that same address. Promise you'll miss me?"

Something twisted inside her. "How long . . . how long will you be gone?" Would their married life be this way? Constant good-byes? With never the sure feeling that Reid was hers or that he would return?

"I'm not sure. There's a possibility I may not be back in time for David and Susan's wedding." He bent his head and took her mouth warmly.

She gazed into his face. She should be glad he was going, shouldn't she? He was a ruthless schemer, a cold-hearted, mercenary man. Then why did she feel so bleak when he went out and closed the door behind him?

184

CHAPTER 9

Fog clung to the windows of the apartment. Foghorns
played their mournful melody out over the water like
hounds baying after an eternally escaping fox. Amanda
stood at the window of the darkening room, watching the
city lights struggle to shine through the mist in distorted,
blurred circles. Beads of moisture formed on the window-
pane, lost their balance, and slid down the glass. Alone,
enclosed in the fog, she felt as helpless, as mindless as they.
Susan had left earlier to dine with David. Her father, after
so many years of obliviousness, had discovered Benita
Ross to be an essential part of his life. He had dressed and
gone out only a few minutes before, telling Amanda some-
what sheepishly that he was taking Benita to dinner.

In the two weeks since he had left, she had not seen nor
heard anything from Reid. She had gone shopping with
Susan and the card had lain in her purse, its crisp white-
ness and dark print a reminder of the man she had cold-
bloodedly agreed to marry, in whose arms she felt anything but cold-blooded. Warmth flooded her cheeks in the
darkness of the apartment. She folded her hands around
her middle, trying to forget the way he could arouse her
with the slightest touch on any part of her body. Even
through the hours of following an indomitable Susan

185

around the city, looking for a wedding gown that suited her, Amanda had only to be touched by the seamstress to remember the way Reid had caressed her and driven her to a depth of wanting and desire she had not thought it possible for her to feel.

Restlessly, she turned away from the window and switched on the lamp on the table next to the velvet chair. She was in limbo, waiting. Only in Reid's presence did she feel alive. Hating him, fighting him, desiring him, gave a strange new impetus to her life. She might have been in a coma that year in New York, waiting. With one afternoon, one kiss, Reid had awakened her. Like a sleeping princess. She shook her head ruefully and sank down on the couch. She was becoming maudlin, crazy. Reid was no prince in shining armor. He was a cold, unfeeling, ruthless man who had proposed to her because he desired her and wanted to have children with her to please his mother. If and when he tired of her . . . *If. When* he tired of her . . . She clenched her fingers into her palms and moaned softly. There was no question that he would. He was an experienced lover, and she was a girl who had never gone beyond a few searching kisses. She had never granted any man the intimacies she had granted Reid. And after their marriage, when he grew tired of her inexpert lovemaking, he undoubtedly would not hesitate to engage in a discreet affair, or even a not-so-discreet affair. They didn't love each other. What would stop him from finding other amusements while she waited at home with . . . *with their children*? The image of a boy with silver-gray eyes and a mop of red hair flashed through her mind. Would she do as other women did, find compensation for the lack of love from her husband in the children they would surely have?

She lay down on the couch, burrowing into the pillows,

feeling a flash of pain. It was an impossible situation, and she had walked into it with her eyes wide open. Except that the time in Owens Valley had confused her. There Reid had donned the garb of a cowboy. Had she unconsciously given him a cowboy's silent strength and integrity? There had always been that aura about such men, as if a male who pitted his wits and muscles against animals and nature had no need of lies and deceit. She must have.

The sharp ring of the doorbell made her sit up. Her heart began to beat against her ribs. Only one person would ring the doorbell with that imperial touch and expect to be received unannounced. *Reid!* She stood up, glad she was still reasonably presentable in the silk blouse, slim skirt, and high heels she had worn to the dress fitting that afternoon. She walked quickly to the door and undid the chain lock without a second thought, strangely eager. But it was Colin Brent who stood in the hallway, immaculate as always in a pale blue suit, his blond hair glistening with moisture, his lips lifted in a smile.

Utter surprise froze the greeting on her lips. He took advantage of her amazement to take the door from her nerveless fingers and close it, imprisoning her inside the apartment with him. Frantically, she groped for a reason he might have come other than to see her. "If you've come to talk to Dad—"

"I didn't," he said flatly, "and you know it."

The tone of his voice frightened her. "He's . . . he's inside, sleeping," she improvised wildly.

"Cut it, Amanda," he said unpleasantly, his eyes lingering where her breasts thrust against the silk blouse. "I know he left long ago." He took a step toward her. "We both know why I'm here."

187

"No," she said huskily, not sure whether she was denying his statement or his intention to take her in his arms.

He shook his head, catching her arm, pulling her toward him. "You know you want this as much as I do."

"No," she said, thoroughly panicked now, bracing her hands against his chest.

"Oh, come off it, Amanda," he said, his voice harsh with impatience. She could feel his breath against her face and smell its odor. She realized with a sinking feeling that he had had something to drink beforehand. "Buchanan pushed me out of his hotel suite that afternoon so you two could be together. Now you're wearing his ring. You can't be the untried little virgin you once were. He must have taught you something." He bent his head and laid his moist mouth on hers. Anger, white-hot and searing, surged through her. She went utterly still, stone cold in his arms. He persisted, trying to pry open her mouth, probing her lips with his seeking tongue. She clenched her teeth and kept her mouth locked, lying in his arms like a mannequin, refusing to incite him by struggling.

He lifted his head, his eyes glinting with anger. His hands were iron-hard on her back. "You haven't changed. You're the same frigid package you always were." He released her, his mouth curving into a sneer. "I thought Buchanan would have warmed your chilly little soul by now." He laughed unpleasantly. "It's no wonder Lisa was such a refreshing change. She was passionate, insatiable right from the beginning." His eyes glittered with contempt and malice. "We went to bed together the first night we met, while you still wore my ring. She found it exciting to be with a man who was engaged to another woman—exciting and amusing."

Amanda's stomach lurched. She stood rigidly, clenching her nails into her palms, hating him with all the strength in her slender body, yet pitying him, too. His love for Lisa had turned him into something less than he had been. "Get out of here," she ordered him huskily.

Her flash of anger and pity infuriated him. "You cold little bitch!" he growled, his voice rough with fury. "You put yourself up on a marble pedestal above the rest of us just because you've never felt a little good, old, honest lust!"

She stood silent, averting her eyes. But he had known her for years and something of the flicker of her eyes must have given him a glimpse of her thoughts. He took a step closer, his eyes glittering with a new, curious light. "Or is it possible you've learned something after all and you've fallen in love with Buchanan?" He stared at her for a long moment, and then threw his head back and laughed, a harsh crack of sound in the still apartment. "That would be funny if it wasn't so pathetic. You're saving yourself for Buchanan. And right now he's in London with my wife." His lips twisted in a sardonic smile, he grasped her upper arms in an iron grip, causing her to cry out in pain. "Don't you know he's marrying you to hide the affair he's having with my wife?"

She stared at him. "I don't believe you."

"Oh, yes," he said savagely. "There is someone in the world Reid Buchanan needs and it's Tom Wallingford. They're together in London, closing a business deal I worked on before Buchanan sacked me. But don't think because her father is there with them that Lisa won't be with Reid. She could conduct an affair under her doting father's nose and he'd never know it. She has. She's been sleeping with Buchanan for years."

Amanda stiffened with anger and pain. Colin shook her

189

as if she were Lisa, and he could take out his jealous anger on her. "She wants to divorce me and live openly with Reid, but she's afraid to, especially since Reid is engaged to you. Which is exactly what Buchanan had planned. Do you think Buchanan will really marry you when he returns?" He laughed again.

His fingers tightened on her arms. Amanda fought the panic that threatened to climb the walls of her stomach to the top of her throat. Colin was obsessed with Lisa, driven over the edge of common restraint by his jealousy. "So you see," he said, his voice husky, "there's no need to save yourself for him."

She fought for calm. "Colin, let go of me."

"No," he said, pulling her closer to him till she felt the pressure of his suit coat against her breasts. "We'll pick up where we left off, Amanda. If you do marry Buchanan, we'll be invited to the same places, see the same people. You'll be a pleasant addition to my father-in-law's dinner parties." He sought her earlobe with his mouth, murmuring in her ear. "He's a photography nut. He collects pictures of San Francisco taken during the years of its history. He has one of Nob Hill after the earthquake." He went on murmuring to her, pressing kisses on her hot, angry face, holding her in the grip of his hypnotic voice, and making her feel caught on the edge of a nightmare. "He loves to show it in his projection room on the three wide screens he had installed. The city looks as if it had been bombed; every building is nothing but empty walls open to the sky." He paused to raise his head and smile down mockingly at her. "Later, when Lisa and Reid slip away to that room to make love in the dark, we can find our own place together. Buchanan won't mind swapping his wife for mine."

She raised one high-heeled shoe and brought its stiletto tip down on the tender spot just above his instep. He yelped with pain and jumped back from her. "What the devil—"

"Get out of here, Colin," she said sharply, her eyes flashing a warning as he stepped closer again. *"Get out!"*

He rubbed his leg, keeping his head tilted to watch her warily. "You stupid little fool." His voice was heavy with contempt. "You deserve everything you get," he snarled. He straightened and stared at her and then limped to the door. "Just remember that I warned you. Don't come crying to me after you've married him and he makes a prize fool of you. You're walking into his trap with your eyes wide open."

She couldn't remember when the sound of a door closing was any more welcome. She sank down on the couch, shuddering, burying her head in her hands. Blood pounded in her brain. Her heart beat wildly. How could she have worked for Colin for three years, been engaged to him for a year, and known so little of his cruelty, his vindictiveness? And how much of what he had said was true? Any of it? All of it? Some stubborn part of her mind rejected it all, told her that Colin was obsessed by Lisa, tormented by her, and driven mad by his own jealousy. Reid might have had affairs with women; he might have enjoyed a brief fling with an attractive actress or model whose own career choice eliminated the possibility of a home and children, but a conniving Reid Buchanan simply didn't fit the picture of the man she had come to know in Owens Valley. That man had treated his mother with an amused deference and warm care, had been tossed ignominiously into the watering place for horses, and had retaliated with a mild threat to her, which had been abandoned the moment Janie had protested. That man had been earthy, real, totally incapable of deceit. She had trusted him implicitly.

And yet, *and yet*! Suppose it *were* true! Suppose after they were married, Reid went on seeing Lisa, went on making love to her. Colin's words echoed in her head. Was Reid with her even at this moment? In her mind's eye, she saw them in a London hotel room, Reid's body, naked and tanned, leaning over Lisa, a Lisa wearing a bright, feline smile on her own red lips and nothing else.

Amanda lifted her head, a searing pain beating in every cell of her body. "No," she cried into the empty apartment. She jumped to her feet. "No," she said again, and the sound came back empty and mocking. She stared at herself in the mirror above the mantel. Even in the dim light, she could see that her hair was disheveled and that her eyes held the same wild look of jealous pain that she had seen in Colin's. She was jealous, wildly, insanely jealous. She stared at her face in the mirror, letting the truth beat over her like the ocean breaking against the headlands. There was only one reason for her jealousy. And that was love. She was in love with Reid Buchanan!

She thrust her hot face in her hands and moaned. She knew then that she loved Reid with a single-minded intensity she hadn't understood at all. She had called it a dozen different things—trust, physical attraction, her response to his sexual expertise, even hate. But it hadn't been any of those. It had been love she had felt in his arms, love, wild and warm and sweet and seasoned with passion, a love that had come so suddenly she hadn't recognized it. She loved him as she had never loved anyone before in her life. Her unconscious mind must have recognized the fact or she never would have agreed to marry him, even for her father's sake. She lifted her head to stare at herself once again in the mirror. She was marrying the man she loved. But he would never love her!

She twisted away from her own image. She couldn't do it, she just couldn't do it! She couldn't marry a man she loved desperately, knowing that he loved another woman! She couldn't take his name and share his bed and have him make her more vulnerable to pain than she had ever been with Colin.

But if she didn't marry him, her father would be ruined. His company would be bankrupt and men who had worked for him for years would be thrown into a job market that was fiercely competitive. Her father would be destroyed. It would be even more cruel now after his hopes had been raised. She knew Reid would not hesitate to use his influence to have all the offers to her father withdrawn.

Her choice was simple, she could save herself or her father. She could marry Reid on his terms: be the hollow receiver of his fleeting sexual interest until he felt Lisa's father had been lulled into believing there was nothing between the two lovers. Then he would return to Lisa's arms. Or she could call him in London now. She could tell him that marriage was impossible, that she was leaving San Francisco. She could get on a plane and go—Where? Where could she go to forget what she had done to her father?

She sank down on the couch, her heart pulling her down like a stone. She would marry Reid. There was no other choice. Her head came up. But he must never know she loved him. She would die first. His laughter, or worse, his pity, would be too much to bear. She stared ahead of her into a night that was heavy with the sound of foghorns and empty of hope.

She felt numb and cold as the day of Susan's marriage

approached and little different when it arrived. She stood with Susan in the room provided for brides in the small church in Olancha and moved and smiled just as any other girl might have whose sister was being married. But one thing kept pounding through her brain. Reid would not be there for his brother's wedding. He had called last night to say that business was keeping him in London. *Lisa was keeping him in London!* Reid had spoken to David and then to Amanda. She had clutched the receiver with cold hands, her responses to his questions monosyllabic. He had rung off abruptly. She had found it hard to act naturally the rest of the evening, knowing that he could not bear to be parted from Lisa even for the sake of his brother. Now she watched Susan pace up and down the room like a caged lion, her gown outlining her small, high breasts, her long silk skirt whispering against the veil as she turned. Amanda was happy that at least her sister was marrying a man who loved her.

Jane said, "Do sit down, Susan." She was regal in gray silk, calm and smiling. "Pastor Evans will be asking the Buchanans to replace the carpeting."

"Is it two o'clock yet, Amanda?" Susan grasped her sister's hand with fingers that were icy.

Amanda nodded. "Almost, darling."

"Do I look all right?" Susan examined herself critically in the floor-length mirror, her head tilted and one hand smoothing her dress while the other held a bouquet of white roses.

"You look lovely," Amanda assured her. "Please try to relax, darling. Think of poor David." She said the one thing she thought would divert her sister. "Think how nervous he must be."

Susan shook her head and wheeled around, making the

bouquet of roses shimmer and tremble in her hand. "He isn't, not at all. He went through rehearsal last night as if he'd been married a million times and memorized my part, too. Oh, Amanda," she cried, "I can't remember anything I'm supposed to do."

The door opened and Janie came in dressed in a yellow gown with a wide ruffle around her shoulders like Amanda's. She carried a wicker basket tied with a yellow ribbon and filled with white rose petals. "They want you, Aunt Jane."

Jane rose. "Chin up, Susan," she said to the nervous bride. "You'll do fine." Her eyes flickered over Amanda in the coppery silk dress that showed off her creamy shoulders in the flattering ruffle. "I find it hard to believe that after all these years of waiting my boys are being married to two lovely girls in a week's time." She moved forward and caught each girl's hand in her own. Tears shone in her eyes. "I want you both to know I couldn't be happier."

"Dear Jane," Amanda murmured huskily. Then the woman was gone. Amanda followed her into the sanctuary as she had been instructed.

After that, Amanda could never recall much about the wedding. It was as if she saw vignettes. Her father, resplendent in his gray evening suit, with Susan pacing slowly down the aisle at his side. Susan, smiling brilliantly at David as she reached the altar and taking his arm, all trace of nerves gone. Robert Conroy, tall, slim, and serious, standing in the place that was to have been Reid's. The warm scent of cedar and roses. The empty feeling in the pit of her stomach when she took Bob's arm to leave the sanctuary after David and Susan had said their vows. She knew that Reid would not be there to share this day. She even tried to forget that in one short week she, too, would be married in this church with only Jane and Josh attending. Her father could not spare another day out of his week, he said, and Susan and David would be honeymooning in Hawaii after flying there in the company plane Reid had reserved for them.

After David and Susan changed and flew down the steps through showers of rice, Amanda went with Jane and Josh back to the ranch house. The phone was ringing when they let themselves in the door.

Jane answered, talked to the caller for a few minutes, and then handed the phone to Amanda.

"I'm sorry," Reid said shortly.

"Don't be," Amanda replied, her voice cool. "I'm sure it couldn't be helped."

"I'll make it up to Susan somehow," he said. Then, "I'll be tied up here for a few more days. Stay at the ranch till I come for you."

For the long space of a moment, she clutched the phone. A million wild thoughts ran through her head. She could tell him that she never wanted to see him again, let alone marry him. She could tell him that she knew about Lisa and that she couldn't—

"Amanda?"

"Yes," she heard her own voice saying. "I'll be here." She put the receiver down in a quick movement. She hoped Josh and Jane would blame the wedding of her sister for the unshed tears in her eyes as she begged off from having coffee in the kitchen. Her escape to the bedroom was more comforting. She wasn't in Reid's room this time. But it didn't matter. Nothing kept him out of her mind and her heart.

He didn't return until the morning of their marriage. He

was barely off the plane and carrying his suitcase into his room before they were in the car riding to the church.

She was jammed next to him in the front seat of Jane's Datsun. Though they were physically close, she felt light-years away from him, the man she was going to marry. Her stomach churned. Jane and Josh rode in the back and chatted easily with each other. She was grateful for their presence. But what could she have said to stop Reid from marrying her?

You don't want that anyway, her mind whispered. *You're so much in love with him, you'll take him on any terms.*

When they walked into the church, she avoided Reid's eyes, afraid he might see the love that burned in hers.

He strode away from her, his back erect in the dark gray suit. She and Jane went to sit in the waiting room where they had been with Susan barely a week ago. She had time to take only one nervous turn over the rug that Susan had trod when a knock sounded on the door. Tears sparkling in her eyes, Jane pressed a cool mouth to Amanda's cheek and went out.

Amanda stepped out and linked her arm with Josh's, glad for his support. She walked down the aisle toward Reid with her head high, but her knees trembled under her. When it was time for Josh to give her in marriage to him, Reid's eyes swept over her with a cool remoteness. His kiss after the ceremony was a perfunctory brush of his mouth over hers. She had married a stranger, a man she didn't know, a man who didn't love her. She must be mad.

When they were driving back to the house, Josh said to his nephew, "I'm glad this marriage business is over. I've got a herd to get up the mountainside."

"Could you use a couple of extra hands?"

"Sure could," Josh said. "Couple more of my boys came down sick. Who were you thinking of?"

"Amanda and me."

Josh squinted, gazing at Reid in the rear-view mirror. "You crazy, son? You and Amanda hardly had a decent wedding. Least you can do is have a honeymoon."

"We are," he said shortly. "Right here in Owens Valley. And Brown's meadow when we get up there."

Jane frowned. "Reid, you can't take Amanda up there for your honeymoon."

"Can't I?" Reid's eyes gleamed. "I've had all the city life I can stand for a while. I need some fresh country air and some privacy. What better place than the cabin?"

Jane snorted. "You've done some outlandish things in your time, Reid Buchanan, and I've never said much. But you can't do this. You can't take Amanda up there."

"Why not?" Reid's tone was lazy. "Amanda is looking forward to it, aren't you, darling?" he asked, as if they had discussed it and agreed in advance. His glance was the exact opposite of his tone, dark and warning. She knew then that her penitence had just begun. He meant to humiliate her, to remind her that she was in his power completely.

Pride lifted her chin while anger made her clench her hands. "Yes, of course," she said smoothly, adding for good measure, "it should be fun."

His face was cool and implacable, but something, a gleam of what might have been admiration for any other woman, shone in his eyes.

They reached the ranch and went inside the house. "Well, you two can take my room tonight," Jane said. "At least you can be comfortable for one night."

"No." Reid's refusal was firm. "I have work to do. I'll

198

be up until we leave using the telephone. Amanda can stay right where she is."

"Reid—" his mother began, a warning tone in her voice.

"Mother," he echoed in exactly the same tone. "Are you so anxious to have your grandchildren?"

Even blunt-spoken Jane retreated in the face of that. "I just thought—"

"I have some last-minute business to take care of," he said, pulling off the jacket of the dark suit he had worn to be married in and sitting down by the phone. "It has to be done tonight or I won't have the next two weeks free."

"I'm surprised you could take the afternoon off to get married," Jane observed tartly.

"I couldn't," Reid shot back. "That's why I have to work tonight."

"Men are nothing but a pack of fools," Jane muttered, frowning. "I'll tell Tessa you're staying for supper, Josh."

CHAPTER 10

It was dark and cool when she felt Reid's hand on her shoulder. She rolled over, not remembering where she was or what had happened. She only knew she wanted to sleep.

"Time to get up, Amanda."

She moaned, thinking it was a cruel joke. "Go away."

His hand slipped under her back. He brought her up and away from the pillow, his face only faintly visible in the night. Still holding her, he reached out to turn on the light. She squeezed her eyes shut and groaned. "What time is it?" she asked, her voice husky. "It feels like the middle of the night."

"It's two o'clock," he answered, his voice low and amused.

Her eyes flew open. She stared up at him balefully. "You're mad."

He shook his head. "You never did like to be roused out of your sleep, did you?" He sat beside her, disturbingly male and attractive in jeans and sheepskin jacket. She was coming awake now, feeling the warmth of his hand through the silk of her nightgown. His other hand lifted to brush a stray lock of red-gold hair from her forehead. "I like the way you look, even at this hour." He kissed her lightly on the mouth and laid her back on the bed. "Get

200

up and get dressed. We're almost ready to leave." He left the room. She got out of bed and slipped into her jeans and shirt and Tessa's jacket, thinking she was the one who was mad.

The kitchen was brightly lit. Tessa was serving the cowboys plates that were heaped with potatoes, pieces of steak, and pancakes laden with butter and syrup. She couldn't eat a tenth of the food she was given. There was much good-natured kidding among the cowboys, who seemed to think it quite normal to get up in the middle of the night and eat enough food to keep a bear through the winter.

Outside, the night air was crisp, the stars close. Everything had been packed the day before except the meat, which Charlie was wrapping in canvas and stowing into the back of the pickup.

The red dome light of the county sheriff whirled through the night, throwing off warning beams to motorists that the road was closed. John barked out orders and opened gates, and the cattle flowed across the road in a red sea, their white faces reflected in the flashing light placid. A forest ranger stood to the left of the herd, a counter in his hand. Pack mules, their loads carefully packed and distributed by the man who had done it many seasons, were loaded into trucks along with the extra horses. Amanda got into a cab beside Reid. They bounced over a five mile stretch of flat desert to the foothills of the Sierra Nevada range that rose in dark ridges against the night sky. Reid told Amanda they would meet the herd later in a fenced-in area called a pack station.

They would be on the trail for two days. The first day the pace was slow. The sun had risen by the time the trail began its ascent through the mountains, but the cattle slowed as the day wore on and lifted dust into the air constantly. Amanda rode on the roan behind the herd, watching her assigned section to see that no cow strayed away from it. She bent and swayed to keep her balance on the horse's back as it picked its way up the mountainside. She was glad for the physical exercise and the task that kept her mind fully occupied. She didn't want to think of what awaited her at the top of the mountain.

By the end of the day, she felt as if she had been severely beaten. Accustomed to riding though she was, she had never spent so many hours in the saddle before. Every muscle in her body ached as she dismounted and walked toward the camp where a fire glowed. The tents had been pitched in the most level places.

She ate her supper sitting on a fallen tree trunk next to Bob Conroy. "Tired?" he asked.

"Are you kidding?" she said wearily, her tone tinged with sarcasm. "I'm ready to go another sixteen hours."

Bob chuckled. "By tomorrow you'll get used to it."

Reid, who had gone to see about the horses, returned. As he pulled her to her feet, she bit back a gasp of pain. She would die before she would admit to him that she felt any discomfort. "Our tent is over there," he said, pointing to a small blue peak that rose from a grassy area close to the fire away from the rest of the tents. "I'm afraid it lacks the proper amenities," he said, his voice carrying the first hint of amusement as they walked toward it. "Shall I watch for you while you—" He nodded his head to the dark undergrowth beyond the light of the campfire.

"I've already been," she said shortly, shaking his hand from her arm and walking toward the tent with as much agility as she could muster.

"Don't you want to wash you face in the stream?" he asked in the same mocking tone.

She turned to face him, staring at his dark form outlined against the flickering firelight, keeping her voice low so that the other cowboys seated around the campfire drinking coffee and talking would not hear. "I'm too . . . I mean, it's too late. I'm going to bed."

She ducked inside the small tent and slipped out of her jeans to crawl into the sleeping bag. Reid waited outside, but then he too came in. He bent himself almost double to accommodate his height to the small tent. She faced away from him, watching the fire flicker against the walls, holding her breath. He said nothing, made no move to touch her. She sighed a small sigh, whether from relief or disappointment, she wasn't sure. She closed her eyes and slept.

By the middle of the next day, she had become accustomed to the numbed state of her posterior. She would feel that way for the rest of her life, she was sure. There had been one hair-raising place on the trail where the rise of the mountain fell away to a sheer drop on the other side. Reid and the men were kept busy urging the cattle through it. It was after that section of trail that she realized there would be no return for her. Reid had planned it all quite deliberately, the endurance test of riding up the mountain to a cabin that was almost inaccessible. She would never be able to leave the meadow without his help. She was trapped, neatly and completely.

Her eyes flashed to him. He rode ahead of her on a fresh horse, a bay. She tried to hate him, tried to keep her eyes away from that lean body swaying in the saddle, tried to shut her ears to the attractive tones of his voice when he talked to the others or gave a command to his horse. But she couldn't. She could only keep his image away by thinking of Lisa, but even that was becoming more and more difficult. Lisa did not seem real here in the mountains with the cattle and the pine trees.

They reached the lush meadow around five o'clock that afternoon. Reid told her that the cabin had been cleaned and made ready, the generator started. They rode to the hitching rail and got off their horses, Amanda biting her lip. Reid took a brass key from his pocket and unlocked the door. The bars at the windows kept the bears out, Reid told her matter-of-factly. Amanda shuddered. The place was immaculate; it had a rough beauty with the voluminous fur rug in front of the stone fireplace and the glow of the pine walls. An ancient stove stood on claw feet and the cabinets gleamed in a knotty-pine gold. She wandered around the room, touching the pine furniture, keeping her eyes away from the double bed that stood in the corner of the room. It was made up with linen and a patchwork quilt in a starburst pattern in reds and blues. A stainless-steel shower cabinet drew her. Curious, she pushed the curtain aside to look in. It appeared clean and operational.

"We'll have hot water in about a half hour," Reid said. "I'll even let you get cleaned up first. Sit down and relax."

She flashed him an angry look that he understood at once. "All right, stand up and relax. I'll go take care of the horses and put the meat in the cooler."

"Where will the men stay?" she asked.

"Most of the boys will go back home," he said. "The few who stay will bed down outside in tents. They know the cabin's going to be off limits for a few days."

"A few days?" she said huskily.

His eyes darkened as they wandered over her slim, tense figure. "Something like that." He turned and was gone.

She walked to a window and gazed out, seeing nothing. Her knees trembled, not entirely from the effects of her days in the saddle. She wandered to another window and saw Reid. He was unloading the canvas-covered packages and putting them into what looked like a large wooden box, which had two sides replaced with screens. He worked nonstop, his muscular body bending and stooping. No wonder the man was lean and agile. Where in heaven's name did he get his energy? After two long days in the saddle, he could still work like this. When the box was full, he threw a canvas cover over it and walked to a pulley. His muscles strained to lift the box high into the air, where it dangled from a log that had been anchored to the roof of the house and a neighboring tree. She realized then that this was their refrigeration, a box lifted into the cool mountain air.

He secured the end of the rope and walked out of her sight to reappear at the door carrying the small suitcase she had packed and a case for himself. His face was dark and unreadable. He moved easily around the cabin, dropping the cases on the stand at the foot of the bed. He turned to her. "The water should be hot now." There was a long, tense silence in the cabin. He shrugged slightly. "I'll go and see if the men are settled."

He went out the door, a grim little smile playing around his lips. Amanda walked quickly to the white enamel cabinet next to the shower stall and found soap and towels. She knew she had been given a reprieve, even if it was only a temporary one. She had spent two days in her jeans and shirt, and she wasn't sorry to strip them off. No shower would ever feel as wonderful as this one would.

The water *was* hot, and though it lacked the pressure she was accustomed to, she luxuriated in it, letting it course over her stiff shoulders and back. She washed her hair quickly and succeeded in getting out, drying herself, and pulling on the caftan she had planned to wear and zipping up its long back zipper before he returned. The lounging garment was one he had bought for her in New York. It was dramatically splashed with diamond-shaped patterns in cream and rust and olive and worked through with gold threads. Somehow the colors complimented her red-gold hair exactly. The handkerchief sleeves fell to a point over her slender wrists. It was provocative because it covered everything, leaving only the slender line of her throat bare. It had a primitive beauty that matched her surroundings and her mood.

She was very busy brushing and drying her hair when Reid returned. When he stepped toward the shower stall, she turned her head away. From the sound of his hasty movements, she guessed that he, too, was anxious for a shower.

Her hair dry, there was nothing to do but lay the dryer on the dresser and move to the window. She stayed there gazing outward, every nerve conscious of Reid's soft steps moving around the cabin.

The darkness enclosed the cabin. The sun had disappeared behind the other side of the mountain, the one they had climbed. She was alone with him; their isolation would not be broken by another living human being. She had come up the mountain. There would be no going down until she had become Reid's wife in every sense of the word.

Suddenly conscious of the quiet in the cabin, she turned. Reid was gazing at her from across the room, a smile playing at the corner of his lips. His shirt was an extravagant flow of turquoise, open to the waist, with loose, full sleeves that buttoned over his wrists. The shirt might have looked feminine on any other man, but tucked into dark, fine-wool trousers, it gave him the look of a marauding pirate.

"I thought since you dressed for dinner, I'd do the same," he said, his voice low with that timbre that sent little flickers down the center of her spine.

"You'll have to tell me how to start the stove," she said, her own voice suddenly husky. "I know it uses wood, but I wasn't sure how to—"

"It's not necessary," he said. "We'll have something easy tonight."

His tone matched her own calm one; it lacked the mocking emphasis she had come to expect from him. He had saved some things out of the cooler, and now he went to the kitchenette and washed and rinsed two plates and two glasses with deft movements. He took out a prepared tray of cold meats and cheeses and a bundle of fluffy rolls from a basket Amanda hadn't noticed before. All Tessa's work, Amanda was sure. From the bottom of the basket he pulled a bottle of champagne.

"From Josh," he said, expertly tapping and popping the cork. Liquid frothed over his fingers. He wiped it away and gathered the bottle and the two glasses in his hands to carry them over to the low table in front of the couch. Another trip made his banquet table complete. He picked up one of the glasses and held it in front of him with a judicial air. On the glass was a golden eagle, its wings nearly gone from repeated washing. "Do you think the champagne will taste the same in these?"

Amanda stared at him, her eyes dark, her face cool.

His mouth tightened. His shrug was casual and his face

207

smooth as he said, "If we're going to eat in front of the fire, I'd better get it going."

He took kindling from the stack next to the fireplace and began to build a fire, his lean body bending and straightening, the turquoise silk billowing around his wrists. The kindling burst into life with one match. At once, the smell of burning pine filled the cabin. The chimney was clean and drew well; flames leaped up from the grate to roar in the quiet, darkening cabin.

Drawn by its light and warmth, Amanda went around the couch and stood behind it, watching the crown of fire dance over the logs Reid had added to the kindling. He was facing her, his body a dark silhouette against the flames. "Come and sit down." The words were quietly spoken, more an invitation than a command.

Amanda walked around and sat in the corner of the couch, slipping her shoes off and curling her feet under her. Her toes were covered by the long folds of her caftan, and a strange sort of calm enveloped her.

Reid sat next to her and handed her an empty plate. She took it. "I would have filled it for you," he said quietly, "but I wasn't sure what you would like. I don't know your tastes yet." He handed her a glass of champagne, his eyes glittering in the reflected light. "To us," he said simply, picking up his own glass and touching hers.

There was a long, still moment. Their eyes met. Her heart seemed to stop beating in her chest. There was huskiness in his voice and a sincerity that put the two words in a world of their own, as if they had been meant so deeply, he could do no more than utter them as lightly as possible.

She drank the champagne watching him. The wine went straight into her bloodstream. She lowered the glass to the

208

table and took a small morsel of food, hoping it wouldn't catch in her throat. She nibbled it, liking the sharp flavor of the cheese. It went down without difficulty. Even though her feet were beside her, a barrier to keep him from sitting too close to her, she was as aware of him as if he were a part of her. He felt so close he might have been her skin.

She held her plate and stared into the fire. Her mind shifted to some primitive level where music played for which there were no words. She knew what the music was. She had heard it before in Reid's arms. It had no words because it needed none. It was a timeless tune that women had sung to men for eons.

She closed her eyes and let the warmth and the scent of the fire enclose her. The sound crackled in her brain. If she concentrated on its primitive lure, she might forget the other pounding inside her, threatening to choke her.

"Look at me, Amanda."

For a moment, she kept her eyes closed. Then she lifted her lashes to stare at his face. It was shadowed against the firelight, his hair a dark aura, his eyes silver as night stars.

He took her plate from her lap, his fingers brushing her caftan along her thigh. The glass was taken from her nerveless fingers. His hands drifted to her feet. He pulled them down gently, the warmth of his hands on her ankles sensual.

One by one he had divested her of her defenses, all the things she had used to keep him at bay and to keep herself from betraying how much she had waited for this moment.

His hands on her shoulders were possessive. Then he said, "You can say no, Amanda."

She was astounded. She wanted to cry out with angry

frustration. He was forcing her to fling her last barrier away and it was the most important one of all. He was forcing her to cast aside the pretense that she had married him for her father's sake, that she was being coerced into his bed. She had needed that, counted on it. She could only hope to hide her love behind his passion, taking his kisses and caresses as if she were responding with the same loveless passion he was giving her. With one simple statement, he had destroyed her!

"Damn you," she cried, thrusting him backward against the cushions. "Damn you to hell!"

She was on her feet and around the couch, pulling clothes from her suitcase in a frenzy.

"*Amanda, for God's sake!*" His hands jerked her around roughly, sending her coppery hair flying.

"Don't touch me." She spat at him with the fury of a cornered cat. I don't want your hands on me *ever!*"

His fingers dug into her shoulders. "Stop lying, Amanda."

"I hate you," she cried. "I loathe you." She stared up into his face, knowing she meant it, knowing she couldn't bear the thought that he had spent almost three weeks with the "passionate, insatiable" Lisa and then returned to marry her as if he were keeping a business arrangement, coolly offering her the choice of whether or not they would make love.

His fingers dug cruelly into her flesh. "Why? Damn you, why?"

"Let go of me," she said, calmer now and gaining control.

But if she gained control, he was losing it. "My wife," he grated, "*a lying, teasing bitch!*" He stared down at her, his bones hard against his face, his eyes brilliant in the flickering light. "I should have known. I should have known you wouldn't have the courage to admit you want me the way any normal woman wants a man. You'll cling to that mothering image if it kills you!"

A numbness spread through her limbs. Her breath came in hard, hot gasps. "I don't have to be your wife. We can have the marriage annulled," she said, fighting to keep her voice low and controlled. "Now."

"So you can run back into Brent's arms?" he said harshly.

The name was like a needle probing her flesh. "You'd like that, wouldn't you?" she flashed. "It would make everything so cozy, so convenient!"

His eyebrows drew into a dark line. "What the hell are you talking about?"

The desire to pierce his self-righteous facade overwhelmed her. "Lisa," she said coolly, watching him. "I'm talking about Lisa."

The firelight danced around the room. The fire popped once explosively. For a long moment, he stood still, staring down at her. Then he smiled, and his smile held comprehension and a cold pleasure. Her heart dropped. She realized suddenly she had given herself away with a single word.

"You're jealous," he said, his voice soft as a serpent's song. "Jealous because you love me."

"How could I love a swine like you," she spat out, "when you've been in London with her for three weeks?"

"And Brent the town crier in my absence." His hands slid down her arms and dropped, making her feel empty and cold.

"Do you deny she was there?" she asked huskily, cursing herself for hoping that by some miracle he would.

211

"No," he said coolly, his eyes never leaving hers.

She shrugged, fighting to hide her pain. She had to convince him that he was wrong, that what he had taken for jealousy was not. "Then it's hardly worth discussing, is it?"

"Oh, yes," he countered smoothly. "It's worth discussing. But—" His voice dropped. "Not just now."

His eyes roamed over her body with a wanton possessiveness that she had to deny. She shook her head and turned away to escape that predatory gleam and her own leaping response. Her loose, copper-colored hair swung about her shoulders and hung in a lustrous cloud around her face.

But turning her back to him was a mistake. A hard male hand clamped itself on her shoulder. The other lifted her hair and found the top of the long zipper at her nape. With one deft movement, he slid it down to the top of her buttocks. She gasped and turned, clutching at the caftan that threatened to fall away from her completely. She found herself in his arms, surrounded by the scent of his clean male body.

"Damn you," she cried angrily, her senses inflamed all the more by the warm hand at the small of her back. It seemed to be sending an explosion of sexual excitement straight through her. "Get your hands off me!"

He smiled a hard, arrogant smile and lifted her into his arms. She kicked and struggled, but his smile only widened. He laid her down on the bed and held her flat, sitting next to her, restraining her with hard hands on her shoulders.

He gazed at her steadily until she was still. Then he murmured, "You once told me it was natural for a woman to want to give herself to a man she loved."

212

There was a long, still moment. She stared up at him wordlessly, wishing for the strength to lie.

"I don't remember," she said, prevaricating.

His eyes burned down into hers. Even in the darkening room she could see the glow of desire in them.

"The truth, Amanda," he said implacably.

She stared back at him, mutinously silent, her heart pounding, her naked skin alive under his hands.

"Actions speak louder than words," he said, extending his arm toward her, turning his wrist so that the pearl buttons that fastened the billowing silk around his arm gleamed up at her in erotic invitation.

She longed to meet his eyes with cool indifference and tell him that she didn't need him or any other man. But while her mind rejected him, her body had a will of its own. Her cold hands were lifting to the buttons, freeing them from their restraints. She finished her task and risked a defiant glance up at him.

Mercilessly, he held out the other arm. This time her fingers faltered temporarily, but the need and ache inside her directed them. When she was finished, he raised her hand to his mouth and kissed her fingers slowly one by one, rewarding them for their courage.

Then he stood and began to undress. She lay watching unashamedly as his hard male body emerged into the flickering light.

When he had finished, he sat down beside her to draw away the caftan from the front of her body. "Beautiful," he whispered, his eyes traveling down the long, pale length of her. "God, you're beautiful."

His hands discovered her, moved over the sleek curve of her throat, explored the slope of her shoulder, encircled the swell of her breast. Waves of delight washed over her.

213

His journey of discovery continued slowly and leisurely, taking her down paths of sensual pleasure she hadn't known existed. She was carried beyond the pain of knowing that his slow, gentle touch told her she did not arouse his passion. He was tender rather than obsessed, gentle rather than violent, as if his mind had assessed her innocence and found it wanting. She was lying in the arms of a man who had made this journey many times before, and she had little hope of arousing his passion. But suddenly it didn't matter. It didn't matter that he gave Lisa his passion and her his gentleness. The only thing that mattered was returning in some small portion the sensual pleasure she was receiving.

She raised herself slightly and ran her hands over his chest. She followed her fingertips with her mouth, pressing small kisses against his neck, the hair-covered skin of his chest. She had accepted his lack of passion, but now, as if he had taken a new tack in the wind, everything changed. He groaned and kissed her deeply, exploring her mouth, taking it with as much passion as she could have ever wanted. Then, as if he could no longer bear to go on kissing her without possessing her, he made her his, his body hard on hers. She felt a bittersweet pain and a momentary release of tension. Then it began to build again in a heart-stopping crescendo to explode in a resounding crash of sensation that shook them both.

The fire had died down, the room was almost dark. The fire within her had died, too, but something told her it was only temporary. Reid's lightest touch would bring it flaming to life again. He lay beside her, his face buried in her hair. "You're getting cold," he said, gently moving her to bring the covers over her. His calm words, his smooth, emotionless handling of her body brought the tears to her eyes. She was still achingly conscious of his slightest touch, and he was matter-of-factly tucking her into bed. He had shared the deepest intimacy with her a man could share with a woman, but he didn't love her.

Reid lifted a lazy hand to trace her shoulder and then let it drift upward to touch her face. His fingertips found the wet trail of tears. "Amanda, my God! I can't have hurt you!"

She turned her face to him. His own was a pale blur in the dark. He gathered her into his arms, holding her close. She lay next to him, hearing his heart thudding under her ear. "You're such a baby," he said, stroking her hair. "All your life you've given love, but you're not quite sure how to take it, are you?"

She thrust herself back away from him in fury. "I wasn't given love."

"No?" She heard the lazy amusement in his voice. "What did you think it was, then?"

"Lust, sex, call it whatever you want to call it. You put the name on it." She made a move to throw the covers back and get up, but his hands pushed her down.

"Are you telling me you don't love me?" The words were quiet and contained.

"No, of course not," she sputtered without thinking. "It isn't me we're talking about. It's you—"

He stopped her with a punishing kiss. He lifted his head and looked at her. "Do you know your eyes are shining up at me like a cat's?"

Angrily, she struggled and half rose. He caught her back, thrusting her against the mattress with iron force. "I love you, Amanda Buchanan, but if you try to get out of this bed one more time, you'll regret it."

She hadn't heard a word he said. She struggled furiously

under his hands. "Let me go, damn you!" she screeched. "Let me go!"

He held her against the pillow, his hands hard on her shoulders. "Not on your life," he said, his voice low and warning. "I missed attending my brother's wedding, worked nonstop for almost three weeks, and rode up this mountain so I could get you where you would listen to me. And you're going to do just that. You're not going anywhere until you realize that I love you more than I thought I could ever love any woman, and that you're my wife because I want you, and that I would have done anything short of murder to get you to marry me quickly. I've told you before, I don't believe in wasting time."

She glared up at him in the dark. "You're lying."

"I don't tell lies," he countered coolly.

"Lisa was with you in London," she said huskily.

"No. She was there with her father."

"Colin believes she's having an affair with you."

"Oh, she's having an affair all right, but not with me. She's taken a fancy to one of the young men her father surrounds himself with. She went to London to be with him. She must have told Colin she was sleeping with me to protect him from suspicion." His voice deepened. "Lisa and I have never been lovers."

"She called you her old flame," she said, her voice low.

Reid's laugh was low and attractive. "She had a crush on me when she was sixteen. She's always called me that. But I've never dated her or made love to her. I've been a friend of her father's far too long to risk hurting him that way." He paused. "I haven't looked at or been with another woman since the day you burst into my office suite."

She lifted a hand to touch his mouth. "I . . . I can't believe it."

He clasped her hand in his and kissed her fingertips. "I have to be honest, darling. I didn't really think about marrying you, not at first. When I saw you sleeping in that chair at the hotel, I knew I wanted to take you to bed and wake up with that hair spread on my pillow. When you came to the ranch, I was elated. I thought you had decided you wanted me, too. I was sure of it when I carried you in my arms that night Josh dumped me in the trough. Then when you did offer yourself and we made love, your sweet passion had already begun to entrap me. The first clue I had to the depth of my feeling for you was when I walked in that stable and saw you talking to Conroy. I was choked with jealousy, and I knew it. But I couldn't let you know. I thought you were still in love with Brent, and I wasn't about to admit my feelings to you." His eyes moved over her flushed face caressively.

"I wasn't in love with Colin ever, really." Her love for Reid made her feeling for Colin seem a pitiful thing. She belonged to Reid. She was his. She had been meant for him as surely as the sun was meant to rise in the morning.

A tender smile tugged at his lips. "I know that now. I didn't then. I walked out of the stable telling myself I couldn't let you become so important to me. I talked to Cathrene deliberately, trying to see how you felt when I paid attention to another woman. You seemed to be absolutely unaffected by it."

She remembered the anger she had felt. "I wasn't. I was devastated. You're such a damned attractive man—I didn't know how I could ever hold you."

"Oh, you can hold me, all right," he growled, and gave her a hard kiss. "Hold me, Amanda."

She ran her hands over the strong muscles of his back and pressed her lips against his bare chest. Her senses soared as the familiar taste and scent of him thoroughly aroused her. "And you weren't going to admit you loved me?" Her teeth found the warm skin of his shoulder and she bit him in mock punishment.

He groaned in pretended pain, lifted his head, and said, "Not till the moment I saw you and that stallion tangled together. I thought my heart would explode. When I tried to help you, I was too late. You lay in my arms like a broken doll, and I knew then that if anything happened to you, nothing else in my life would mean a damn. I ached to tell you how much I loved you." He stopped speaking and probed her mouth with the tip of his finger. "The doctor said you were all right, and I was euphoric. You were still asleep. So I decided to call your father first. Then I was going to tell you that I loved you."

"And, instead, you threatened me with my father's financial ruin."

He smiled ruefully. "Do you have any idea how I felt? For years, I avoided any kind of permanent relationship with a woman because I'd never found one who cared a damn about anything but the luxuries my wealth would give her. Then you walked into my life, and you were so loyal and loving to those around you that I couldn't believe you were real." His eyes glittered down into hers. "One telephone call shattered my illusion. I had fallen hard only to find out you were as conniving as any other female. I stood at that window wanting to murder you. But I knew I couldn't let you go."

"Reid, I never meant to . . . to bargain with you sexually. I . . . I must have loved you from the first moment I saw you."

"And I you, darling." He kissed her, a light, unsatisfactory caress. "As long as we're going to have the truth

218

between us you must know I could never have stood by and watched your father suffer in any way. I set the wheels in motion for him to receive that Sausalito job the evening of that first day I kissed you."

"Reid!"

He touched her face gently. "I think I knew then he was going to be my father-in-law as well as David's even though I was telling myself I only wanted you physically." He smiled at her. "As it was, I couldn't wait to get you to the church and make you my wife."

"I thought you were working your marriage in between business calls," she teased, smiling at him. He raised her hand to his mouth and bit the tip of her finger in mock punishment.

She cried out. He smiled at her unsympathetically. "Serves you right," he said huskily. "You should have known how much I loved you."

"How could I," she said, smiling. "I was too busy hiding my feelings for you. Even here I . . . I thought you were forcing me to admit I loved you because you wanted to humiliate me."

"Darling, no! Oh, God, no. I love you desperately. But that wasn't enough." His voice took on a husky timbre. "I had to know that you loved me, too."

Amanda touched the soft, vulnerable spot at the base of his throat. Strength and vulnerability. Reid had them both. He could be tender because he was strong. She knew that now. "I thought you didn't care for me because you were so . . . gentle." She hesitated and then raised her sparkling eyes to him. "You're a virile man, darling, and I expected passion."

His eyes glittered in the dim light. "So my love-making

didn't meet your expectations." He laughed softly. "We'd better try it again, then, hadn't we?"

A soft flush warmed Amanda's cheeks. His eyes moved caressively over her, and then he bent and took her lips with all the passion she could have wanted. The fire gave one last crackle and subsided into dying embers. But for Amanda and Reid love flamed to a new and glorious height.

LOOK FOR NEXT MONTH'S
CANDLELIGHT ECSTASY ROMANCES™

When You Want A Little More Than Romance—

Try A Candlelight Ecstasy!

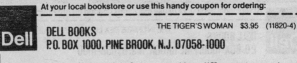